HaNNIE

by
Barbara Luetke-Stahlman

Butte Publications, Inc.
Hillsboro, Oregon, U.S.A.

HaNNIE

© 1996 Butte Publications, Inc.

Editors: Connie Knepper, Ellen Todras
Cover: Anita Jones
Page Design: Anita Jones
Photos courtesy of: Barbara Luetke-Stahlman
Map courtesy of: One Mile Up

Butte Publications, Inc.
P.O. Box 1328
Hillsboro, Oregon 97123-1328
U.S.A.

ISBN: 1-884362-15-X
Printed in U.S.A.

Foreward

This story is loosely based on the life of Hannah Luetke-Stahlman, now 12 years old, who lives in Olathe, Kansas. Some parts of the story are real - like the names of her family, relatives, pets, friends, teachers, school, and the trips she takes. It's true that she has an older hearing sister and two younger sisters who are deaf. The pictures in this book are taken from our family albums and are of Hannah's real family and friends.

Some parts of this book are invented - like the dialogue, the explanation of Hannie's feelings, and what she is thinking. This is because the book is written by her mother and how can one person truly know what anyone else is thinking?

Hannie's family members and many of her friends sign in English. Sometimes they speak when they are signing and sometimes they don't. To show this in the book, I have used regular type to indicate speech and capital letters to indicate signing. I didn't distinguish between sentences that are signed or both signed and spoken. For example, consider these two sentences:

1) I'll go home now. (spoken)
2) THAT'S OK WITH ME! (signed, or both signed and spoken)

There are lots of good books about signing and deafness written for children. If you are interested in reading more about these topics, ask a librarian, or write to this press and request a book catalog:

The Gallaudet University Press
7th and Florida NE
Washington, D.C. 20002

Barbara Luetke-Stahlman
Hannie's Mom
1996

Dedication

To Lydia Moore (mentioned in Chapter 3: "September") who died before ever knowing that I had written about her as a part of the Hannie project. Lydia was 38 years old and a doctor in Kansas City when she died in a car accident in August, 1994. At the time of her death, she had over 3,000 patients, most of them poor. She served many people with AIDS and many who were Hispanic. Lydia was a birth-right Quaker and a model of compassion and caring; over a thousand friends attended the memorial service held after her untimely death. The service lasted for over two hours as many individually shared their memories of this remarkable woman. Lydia had learned to sign her name and communicate some simple concepts to our deaf girls, who were members of her Meeting (church). She was much loved and is much missed by our family.

Acknowledgements

I would like to thank Jean Andrews, author of The Flying Finger Club books (Gallaudet University Press and Northern State University Foundation Press) and Mary Abrams (editor of Perspectives at Gallaudet University), both of whom encouraged me to write about raising my girls. I would like to thank Breeze Luetke-Stahlman, Marcy Coon, and Anna Higgins, who provided honest feedback about the early drafts of the first chapters and encouraged me to talk with elementary-aged children about the project. I would like to thank Sandy Morris, a teacher at Scarborough School, who allowed me to read chapter drafts to her fourth-grade class. Finally, I would like to thank Kent, Breeze, Hannah, Mary Pat, and Marcy Luetke-Stahlman and the friends and relatives who are mentioned in these pages. Without their love and encouragement there would not have been memories on which to base this story.

Table of Contents

Chapter 1

July

*I*t was the fourth of July. Hannie sat on a blanket in the darkness beside her cousin, Jessie, and looked at the night sky. There were few stars and only a sliver of moon above her in the dark Pennsylvania night. She wondered what her friends back home would be doing tomorrow – which was her birthday.

Darn, she thought, we seem to be traveling on my birthday every year. She looked at her family sitting around her. Here were her mother and father, older sister, and two younger sisters. She was a "middle child" - coming after Breeze who was 13, and before Mary Pat who was 6, and Marcy, who was 4. Also sitting on this Pennsylvania hillside was her favorite cousin, Jessica, and many other cousins, aunts, and uncles.

Suddenly, Jessie jabbed Hannah's right side. "Ouch," yelped Hannah. She stared at her cousin in surprise and irritation.

"Want to go get a drink down there?" Jessie smiled sweetly and pointed to a concession stand down the hill.

Hannah looked quickly around her. There seemed to be a million people sitting on this hill in central Pennsylvania, waiting for the fireworks to start. Hannah knew only the small group of relatives that occupied the blankets nearby. The concession stand looked a very long way off in a confusing sea of people.

"Do you think we can get there and back before the fireworks start?" Hannah didn't want Jessica to think that she was nervous about leaving their group. But then, after all, it was dark.... If we get lost, Hannah thought to herself, we'd never find our way back. But on the other hand, it did sound like an adventure - something her parents might not normally allow her to do. Amazing, Hannah sighed to herself, Mama and Daddy have let me do so many new things this summer!

The girls smiled at each other and jumped up simultaneously. Their sudden movement startled Marcy, Hannah's youngest sister, who was deaf. Marcy lost her balance and tumbled out of her squat position and down the hill several feet. She rolled into the back of another cousin and stopped, her feet in the air and her big brown eyes staring widely up at Hannah. Everyone around her couldn't help but laugh at the startled child. Then, before Hannah and Jessie could be on their way, the first firecrackers exploded in the sky. The girls giggled and plopped back down. Marcy crawled back up the hill and snuggled in the safety of Hannah's arms.

"FIRECRACKERS...LOOK!" Hannah signed and pointed up into the dark. Marcy couldn't hear the explosion but she was dazzled and delighted by the colors, sparkling and dropping against the black night sky. She had been adopted in January, just six months ago, from Bulgaria, a country far away across the Atlantic Ocean, and this was her first experience with a Fourth of July celebration.

"LOOK! LOOK!" The little girl signed back, tapping Hannah again and again and pointing in amazement.

As the three girls watched the colorful explosions in the night sky, Hannah felt warm and happy. She snuggled under the blanket, holding Jessie's hand on her left side and hugging Marcy on her right. This was a summer night to remember! Hannah was on vacation, surrounded by the family she loved. And tomorrow, she sighed and laid back on the blanket, tomorrow is my birthday and I will be nine years old!

When the fireworks ended, Jessie and Hannah held hands as they walked back to the car. It was a short drive to the motel where all the reunion families were staying. Yet, before the family van pulled into the parking lot, all the girls were asleep.

Mama kissed Hannah awake, tugging gently on her arm. "Come on, Birthday Girl. We need to get you to bed."

As Hannah stumbled out of the van, she saw

her Grandma Bette approaching.

"Do you and Jessie want to sleep in my room tonight, honey?" Grandma Bette asked. Hannah grinned sleepily. Her family of six was sharing one room. There were suitcases, shoes, towels, and people from one wall to the other. A room with only Grandma and Jessie would be heavenly!

"Sure!" She and Jessie were suddenly wide awake, running to get their pj's and toothbrushes.

It turned out that sleeping in Grandma's room was a good deal for several reasons. First, Grandma took the cousins to breakfast as soon as they were up the next morning. Hannah only had to share her grandmother with Jessie - not any of her three sisters, Breeze, Mary Pat, and Marcy. And she didn't have to try to eat and sign at the same time. Hannah's family signed because both Marcy and Mary Pat were deaf and couldn't hear speech clearly. Signing and eating at the same time was a real trick and Hannah often dropped food in her lap!

And Grandma let Hannah and Jessie order anything they wanted! That never happened when her big family went out to eat. As Grandma Bette sipped her coffee, Jessie gave Hannah a shiny rock she had found at the park as a birthday present. "Keep it in your pocket to remember me," she said. Grandma surprised her with stationery with little bears printed on the top of the paper. "To write me lots of letters," Grandma said.

Breakfast was fun for another reason, too, because Grandma Bette explained their family tree. She drew lines on her napkin from the names of relatives to show the girls who was related to whom. The part with Grandma, Hannah, and Jessie looked like this:

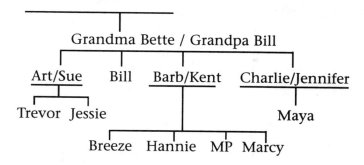

Grandma Bette / Grandpa Bill
Art/Sue   Bill   Barb/Kent   Charlie/Jennifer
Trevor Jessie   Maya
Breeze   Hannie   MP   Marcy

By the time the girls finished their special birthday breakfast, Mama and Daddy had Hannah's sisters fed (they had been eating all week in their hotel room!) and the van was packed and ready to go. Hannah's family was continuing their vacation, leaving for upper New York state for three days on Lake Erie with Mama's friend, Betsy.

Hannah found it hard to say good-bye to her aunts and uncles and cousins. Her family had never held a reunion before and she had had a wonderful time swimming in the motel pool with relatives she seldom saw. Jessie's daddy, Uncle Artie, had tossed her up over his head, again and again, and let her splash back into the water. He never seemed to get tired. They had also been to an old-fashioned family picnic in the park where Grandma and her brother and sisters had played long ago as children. Everyone played catch and frisbee and softball. They ate salads and chips and talked, catching up and enjoying each other's company.

Hannah cried when she hugged her Grandma Bette good-bye. Grandma seemed sad, too. Grandma Bette lived in Florida and Hannah's family didn't see her very often.

Hannah couldn't even look in Jessie's eyes when she said good-bye to her favorite cousin. She probably doesn't think I'll miss her much, Hannah thought. But she was missing her already...even as Daddy pulled the van out of the motel driveway. Well, anyway, sighed Hannah, rubbing the stone Jessie had given her, I'll get to see her again next year.

Hannah liked traveling in the van. Her family had taken summer car trips for as long as she could remember. The past three summers they had camped and ridden horses in Montana, traveled to North Carolina for a week of "Quaker Camp," and seen Niagara Falls from a little blue boat called the Maiden of the Mist. This year Daddy had bought a full-sized van to travel to the reunion. It had a TV and a VCR and the radio or cassette tapes could be played through individual headsets, so Mama and Daddy weren't bothered by the older girls' music. Hannah's parents preferred to talk while they drove and not to listen to the rock music that Breeze and Hannah enjoyed. Marcy and Mary Pat usually colored or played with their Barbie dolls. They could spend hours signing back and forth to each other, creating a pretend Barbie-land right there in the van!

In no time at all, Hannah's daddy was turning down the bumpy gravel road following the directions that Mama's friend, Betsy, had given them to her cottage. Lake Erie looked as huge as an ocean. The cottages that lined the road were small and painted in lots of pretty colors. They reminded Hannah of the wooden blocks that Marcy played with at home.

Daddy was driving and Mama was reading the directions. They found the cottage they thought must be Betsy's and were relieved to see Betsy in her front yard, sitting in a lawn chair and waiting for their arrival. Hannah immediately noticed a girl about her age standing behind Betsy.

Everyone piled out of the van, pleased that the day's ride was over. When Hannah saw Mama hugging her good friend, she suddenly felt shy. She lingered in the back of the van, missing Jessie all over again.

At first, no one seemed to notice. Mama was introducing Betsy to Marcy and Mary Pat because Betsy had never seen the little girls before. Betsy ooooed and ahhhed over Hannah's big sister, Breeze, whom she had not seen since Breeze was two. When Mama and Betsy were in school together, Breeze had called her "Beppie." Now Breeze was 13 and Betsy couldn't get over it.

All of the sudden, Betsy looked through the van window and spotted Hannah. "Is that you, Hannah? Come out and meet Alliyson. She's just your age!"

Hannah regained her courage when she saw Daddy interpreting Betsy's comments for Mary Pat and saw that Mary Pat was signing and complaining, "WHY DOES HANNAH HAVE A SPECIAL FRIEND?" Mary Pat had been jealous of Hannah and Jessie at the reunion and could hardly bear the thought of once again having to share Hannah with someone else.

Hannah knew that she was lucky to find someone her age at Betsy's cabin. She giggled and slipped out of the van into Betsy's hug.

"Hannah, this is my niece, Alliyson. She is nine...just like you." Hannah beamed at Betsy. She was new to being nine and pleased that Betsy knew her age.

Alliyson was a tall, tan girl. She looked like fun. "Do you want to go to the beach?" Alliyson asked Hannah.

"Sure," Hannah replied. She glanced at Mary Pat and smiled mischievously.

Mary Pat looked at Mama, her eyes big with concern. "YES," signed Mama. "WHY DON'T ALL YOU GIRLS GO WITH ALLIYSON. DAD AND I WILL UNPACK THE VAN AND GET YOUR THINGS SETTLED IN THE COTTAGE WHILE YOU'RE GONE."

Hannah frowned - Mary Pat smiled - and the group was off.

For three glorious days no one took a bath, wore shoes, or ate regular meals. The mornings were spent taking long walks among the cottages or down the shoreline, where they collected smooth pieces of green and blue glass that had been washed up on the beach by the waves. In the afternoons the girls played in Lake Erie, built sand castles, and sunbathed. Marcy and Mary Pat were freed of their hearing equipment and everyone wore swim suits all day.

Alliyson and Hannah quickly became buddies. Their relationship didn't feel exactly like hers with Jessie or her school friends back home, but she was a new and comfortable friend, just the same. Hannah felt relaxed knowing that she could spend the day with someone who liked many of the same things she did. Alliyson knew lots of card games and songs. She patiently taught the girls the rules to a game called "Kings in the Corners" and Hannah was secretly proud that she learned it as fast as Breeze did. Alliyson would smile and gesture to Mary Pat so she could understand a little bit about the game, too. Hannah liked that Alliyson made this kind of effort and appreciated not always having to interpret. Alliyson even found a job for little Marcy, who pushed and shoved to be by her side so she would be ready to cut the cards before each round of play.

But all too soon, Hannah's family was packing the van again. This time they would be going back home, stopping near Indianapolis, Indiana, on the way. Hannah couldn't decide what had been her favorite part of being with Betsy and Alliyson at the Lake Erie cottage. Maybe it was the day all the girls had pretended to be models and posed on a big piece of driftwood. Or perhaps her favorite time had been the night Betsy built a blazing bonfire on the beach and they toasted marshmallows in the dark. Hannah had loved everything; eating at the picnic table in the kitchen, walking the shoreline with Mama and Daddy, and sleeping in the loft with all the children in one, big room.

But now the family was on the road again. Hannah passed the time reading a book about a gang of kids called the Signing Fingers Club, but she soon fell asleep. It was almost lunch time when she

woke to Marcy tapping on her shoulder. Her family stopped for a quick picnic lunch and was soon back on the road. By dinnertime they were a little bit south of Indianapolis and near their destination. They were going to stop for a lasagna dinner at the home of the Fores family. Hannah had never met them.   The Fores had adopted a little girl that Hannah knew only from pictures. Her name was Vara and she lived in Bulgaria with Marcy before Vara and Marcy came to the United States.

      The Fores had adopted Vara just like Hannah's family had adopted Marcy. Vara wasn't deaf, but she did need heart surgery and was going to have it later in the year. Hearing Mama and Daddy talk about Vara and the Fores got Hannah thinking about adoption. She remembered the time before Marcy was her sister, when she had only had two sisters, and Mary Pat had been the youngest. Mary Pat had been adopted, too, but Hannah had been too young to remember that. She could remember the day Marcy arrived at the airport with Mama. The little girl had been pale and confused, although she smiled at her new sisters and tried to communicate through gestures. Adoption, Hannah decided, was something parents did when they wanted children who didn't need diapers and could sleep through the night. At least that was how it had been with Mary Pat and Marcy.

Hannah glanced over at Marcy. She really loved the little, brown-eyed girl who had come to be a part of their family. Marcy smiled back. Hannah knew Marcy loved her; really loved her. She always found Hannah when she was upset or wanted a special hug. Now Hannah watched her sister twist a piece of string around and around in her fingers as the van moved along. Marcy could entertain herself for the longest time with almost nothing at all! When she had lived in the orphanage in Bulgaria she had none of the things that Hannah took for granted, like toys or crayons or dolls. She had never learned to ride a bike or jump rope until she came to America. And now she was about to see her old friend, Vara. How odd, Hannah sighed, she doesn't understand that wonderful thing is about to happen!

Daddy, who was driving, began to explain to Marcy about seeing Vara. Hannah knew that Marcy couldn't see his signs from her seat in the back, so she repeated what Daddy was saying so Marcy could understand. Hannah and Marcy spelled Vara's name over and over until the family arrived at the Fores house. When they parked the van, Mama turned and signed to the girls. "I WANT YOU ALL TO STAY BACK AND LET MARCY HAVE HER TIME ALONE AT FIRST WITH VARA. THEY HAVEN'T SEEN EACH OTHER FOR OVER A YEAR NOW AND IT MAY TAKE A WHILE FOR THEM TO REMEMBER ONE ANOTHER. AND DON'T LAUGH OR COR-RECT VARA IF SHE CALLS MARCY "ANA." MARCY IS ANA TO HER...THAT WAS MARCY'S NAME IN

BULGARIA. IT'S FINE TO LET VARA CALL HER THAT FOR TONIGHT."

Hannah watched through the van windows as Marcy and Mama rang the doorbell and waited as Vara tugged open the door. Vara was five, a year older than Marcy, but she wasn't much bigger. Both girls had short, dark hair. When they saw each other, they hugged and giggled. "V-A-R-A" Marcy fingerspelled back to Hannah. Marcy's excited smile made Hannah feel warm all over.

Soon Dad gave the sign for Breeze, Hannah, and Mary Pat to get out and join the Fore family. Everyone was introduced and then settled down for dinner. There were no girls in the Fore family...well, except for Vara... and she was busy with Marcy. At first Hannah felt a bit bored, and a little lonely. She decided to enjoy watching Marcy and how much fun she was having with her special friend. When she got tired of that, she sat back on the couch and dreamed of being home in Kansas. And, in another day, she was there!

Chapter 2

August

*H*annah's family was only home for a week before they were packing up the van once again. They were going to Madison, Wisconsin, and then north to Steven's Point, Wisconsin, to Suzuki Violin Camp. Both Hannah and her older sister Breeze had played violin and gone to Suzuki camp for many years.

It was always on a Sunday that the family passed through Madison, and they traditionally stopped first at Grandma Rita's apartment on the west side of Madison and then at Grandpa Bill's on the east side of town. Grandma Rita was Daddy's mother and Grandpa Bill was Mama's father.

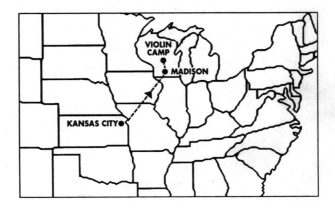

Neither grandparent had a very large home. When Hannah and her Daddy, Mama, and three sisters all sat down in the living room at Grandma Rita's house, the room seemed to shrink. The furniture was beautiful; there were always fresh flowers and interesting things to look at. Before long the girls wandered off to browse in Grandma's refrigerator and check out the pantry. The older girls knew from years of visiting that Grandma always bought fun cookies for them to try and loaded them up with boxes of crackers and treats to take with them to violin camp.

After a good visit, the family would travel across town to Grandpa Bill's. The children sat quietly for about 20 minutes while the adults talked. Then they started to giggle and turn circles in his swivel chairs. Mama gave them a cold stare and suggested that they go to the kitchen for drinks. After that, Mama was still talking with her dad, so the children were sent to the back bedroom play with the pennies Grandpa kept in a big jug. Hannah liked Grandpa's back rooms. The girls loved to make elaborate designs and patterns with Grandpa's pennies and Hannah liked to look at the pictures and diplomas on his walls, too. Well, for a while anyway.

When their parents were exhausted from trying to keep the girls clean, quiet, and polite, Mama, Breeze, and Hannah dropped Daddy and the little girls off at a friend's home and continued north, to Steven's Point. With just the "women" in the van, as Mama called them, the two hours flew by quietly. Hannah took a nap while Mama sang to "oldies but goodies" on the radio. She really didn't have a half bad voice but Hannah hated to encourage her for fear of having to listen to Mama sing even more. Any indication of approval and Mama

14

would sing louder, adding signs, swaying and rocking. It amazed Hannah that Mama could remember the words to all those songs. Will I be like Mama when I am a mama someday? wondered Hannah as she curled up in her captain's chair.

Eventually Mama turned the van off the highway and headed down the boulevard to the University of Wisconsin-Steven's Point. That's where Violin Camp was held!

Hannah's family always stayed in the same dorm as their friends from Sycamore, Illinois, where they had lived for six years before moving to Kansas. Rachel had been Hannah's best friend in Sycamore. This year Rachel's mom was sharing a room with Rachel's two younger brothers and Rachel and her little sister Leah were in a room beside them. They were across the hall from Mama, Hannah, and Breeze.

Once everything had been carried to their dorm rooms, Hannah started to unpack her clothes, putting shorts in one drawer of the old, worn dresser, and tops in another. It was hard to believe that some college-age girl spent an entire school year in this tiny, cramped room - with a roommate! Hannah thought about her comfortable, big bedroom back home that she had all to herself, with its rich carpet, painted bookshelves, and ample closet space. Her dresser, passed down to her from her Mama's grandmother, was in tons better shape than the one in which she now organized her tops and shorts.

That Sunday night there was a huge "play in" with all the students at camp. The children stood in a group and were led through a variety of songs by their teachers. Some of these teachers Hannah recognized; some were new to her. She was

15

watching an instructor now as she knelt and waited for a group to finish playing a Book 5 song. She was in Book 4 and recognized the music, the first movement to a concerto, but couldn't play it yet. Next, a teacher was introduced to play Witches Dance and Hannah popped to her feet. It was fun to see how many songs she knew how to play, allowing her to remain standing. But is was even more fun to watch very young, but very expert boys and girls stand to play difficult songs. Hannah noticed a boy in front of her who looked about six years old. He played as if each song was a major dramatic performance. Well, Hannah admitted to herself, he is very good. Watching the little ham inspired Hannah to become a little more dramatic, and she laughed at herself as she played with the group and enjoyed the evening.

This past year Hannah had often thought about not playing the violin at all anymore, but tonight she felt refreshed and ready to go as she turned her attention to Mrs. Aber, the founder of Suzuki Violin Camp. Mrs. Aber was giving instructions to all of the players. The children were to march in four lines behind certain teachers, following them wherever they went. The students marched through the groups of parents assembled on the hill, all the while playing the four variations of "Twinkle, Twinkle, Little Star." Hannah waved up to the spot where her mother was sitting with Rachel's mom, Robin. They waved back, enjoying the spectacle.

Monday classes started right after breakfast. Hannah was in an "A" class with three other girls who were all nine and also going into fourth grade in a few weeks. One was from California, two from Illinois, and she, of course, told them she lived in

Kansas. "Like Dorothy in The Wizard of Oz?" asked one girl. Hannah smiled tolerantly. Why was that old movie all that people ever knew about Kansas?

Everyone in her A class went on to a "B" class an hour later. It was fun to see the kids roller-skating, walking, and skateboarding all over the college campus. Hannah strapped her violin to her bike and rode to her next class, humming the music her group had just practiced. As she walked into B class, she saw that Rachel was there, too, and they stood together and tuned. Before long, Ann Montzka, their teacher, had them laying on the floor or standing on one foot to play, bending and bowing, playing with upside down bows and lots of other tricks. Some of the parents looked like they were trying to figure out the purpose of these unusual drills, but the rest were buried in novels or stitchery.

Mama came dutifully to each class, but she paid more attention to the work she always brought along than to the class. This summer she was working on a book, and the expression on her face made her

look like she was far, far away. Hannah would
sometimes see her snapping back into reality, looking
around to catch Hannah's eye. It was wonderful to
have even this much of Mama without sharing her
with her younger sisters! Even though Hannah
found herself missing her Daddy, a week-long break
from her little sisters was a treat!

After B class, the girls were on a lunch and
then a practice break. Hannah was very thankful
that her Daddy had helped her practice her review
songs in the weeks before coming to camp. If the
instructor in her C class had them play an old Book
3 song, she was ready! It was a good feeling to
know she could hold her own and she was proud of
herself. She and Rachel went without mothers to
their C class, the last class of the afternoon.

At three o'clock, Rachel and Hannah were
finished with violin lessons and off to dance class,
which they were dreading. "We'll probably have to
dance with boys and learn a lot of old, stupid
dances," Rachel had said.

"Oh, boy," Hannah sighed in Rachel's direction, "I really hope I don't have to dance with a boy,
Rach." Rachel looked up. From the expression on
her face, it was obvious to Hannah that Rachel had-
n't heard her.

Their teacher was a real live wire. "Can you
tie your shoes while you lay on your stomach?"
asked Rachel. Hannah looked at her and frowned;
she decided to ignore the question. Sometimes she
wasn't sure if Rachel was serious or pulling her leg.
She didn't want to look like she cared.

The dance class was held in a huge room
with mirrors lining all four sides and a wooden
floor worn smooth from many years of dancers'
feet. Hannah could see right away that there were

only a few boys. "Grab a partner," the instructor called. Hannah took Rachel's hand in relief.

"We will start by learning to dance to a 15th century minuet. Then I'll teach you moves to "Jump" and a '50s song, too, OK?" she asked. But she didn't wait for an answer. Before long, she had the class dancing a passable minuet. "Now look snooty, please," she called out over the music. Listening to the tempo of the music and the moving with the dance, it was easy for Hannah to imagine that she was dressed in a long, hoop-skirted satin gown from centuries ago. She could almost feel the long gloves on her arms and the black satin slippers on her feet. She and Rachel tried hard to look like sophisticated, 15th century snobs.

With hardly a moment to rest, the music changed, and the girls jerked and twisted to the pop song "Jump." "This beats violin classes by a mile!" Rachel shouted over the music. Hannah felt like she was the star of a dance contest! She and Rachel learned the steps easily and were asked to come up front so others could follow them. At the end of the lesson they also learned the beginning steps to "Rock'n Robin."

"Now, class," said the teacher, "Wednesday is the talent show, you know." Of course, all of the students who had been to camp before knew about the talent show. It was a fun event, and the best part was that no one was allowed near a violin! Instead, kids tumbled, danced, sang, or did ridiculous acts, sometimes to tease their teachers. Often the teachers put on skits to the delight of their students. Everyone enjoyed a playful break from the hard work of lessons and practice sessions.

"If you would like to dance with a group for 'Rock'n Robin' you need to go to the Salvation

Army store and put together a costume that looks like the '50s." Hannah and Rachel looked at each other. They were definitely going to need some parental cooperation for this assignment. As soon as class was over, the girls ran full-speed back to the dorm. "Mommmmm!" they both screamed together as they neared their rooms.

Hannah's Dad arrived from Madison with Mary Pat and Marcy on Wednesday. Almost before he was out of the car, Hannah and Rachel had him back in it, heading to the Salvation Army store. There they found some plaid skirts, pastel blouses, and saddle shoes. Hannah felt super! They had practiced "Rock'n Robin" about a million times. Rachel's mother was going to help them fix their hair while Breeze babysat for the youngest kids. Mama had even agreed to let Hannah wear make-up! "Just some lipstick and a little blush," were her exact words. Hannah was so excited she could hardly eat dinner.

The crowd from Sycamore, Illinois, headed over to the gym for the talent show right after dinner to reserve a big section of seats. When Hannah and Rachel came out on the stage, family and friends from Sycamore were right there in front to cheer them on. Mama interpreted for Mary Pat and Marcy so they would understand what was being said and sung. The music started and Hannah and Rachel whirled into their Rock'n Robin routine. The audience loved it! Parents were clapping and kids were swaying in their seats. Hannah peeked at her parents, who were smiling back proudly. This was great!

On Thursday, Daddy and Hannah took her former teacher Ann to lunch. Ann had been Hannah's teacher in Sycamore. She was young and pretty, and they all talked about Sycamore, about Hannah's violin teacher in Kansas, and the new songs she was learning.

Hannah talked a little bit, but mostly she listened to the two adults. She watched the soft wave of Ann's hair bob as she listened to her gentle voice. She loved that voice...Ann had been a good teacher and Hannah missed her. If Hannah hadn't understood how a piece was supposed to sound, Ann would tell her a story to help her play a part softly or loudly, or she would make up lyrics to help her keep the beat. She had challenged Hannah and kept her accomplishments with music separate from Rachel's.

Once Ann had confided in Hannah that she used to compete with her sister when she was about Hannah's age. She told Hannah that it can make you work harder when you compete a little bit, but she also reminded Hannah that in the Suzuki method the emphasis was on each child's own progress and improvement. The story almost felt like a secret, and Hannah thought about it whenever she felt herself more concerned with what Breeze or Rachel were able to play than with her own work.

Actually, Hannah didn't have as much of a problem with the concept of "no competition" as her mother. It seemed like Mama was always asking who was on which song and whether the girls wanted to take extra lessons. The pressure bothered Hannah a lot and one day Hannah had just come right out and asked Mama to let up. After that Mama stopped asking about other kids so much and even went to parent classes at camp to learn more about the values of the Suzuki method of teaching.

By Friday of camp week, Hannah was really tired and she was ready for a break from her violin. As soon as classes were over, her family was going camping with friends from Madison. Hannah was trying to finish packing in between her lessons. This was a challenge because she was also keeping her distance from her mother. Mama was yelling and directing and trying to get all the bikes, food, and clothes organized and reloaded in the van.

Hannah would definitely be giving Mama a yelling mark on the calendar for today. She and Mama had worked out a deal; every time Mama yelled, Hannah was to make a mark on the calendar in her room. At the end of the week, she counted up the marks and reported the total to Mama. Hannah knew that Mama didn't like herself much when she was yelling. Hannah could remember a time when Mama rarely yelled; but then there had been a move to a new state, Daddy out of work for four months, Marcy's adoption and the yelling had gotten worse and worse. It had been Mama's idea to mark the yelling on a calendar. The system seemed to be working and Hannah was proud that she and her mom could help each other solve a problem.

With Mama and Hannah in the car and Daddy, Breeze, and the little girls in the van, the family left Violin Camp early Friday afternoon and traveled until dinnertime. "Are we almost..." Hannah called to her mom from the back seat about seven o'clock. Mama looked back at Hannah through the rearview mirror to see why she hadn't finished her sentence. Hannah was pinching her nose and holding her breath. "Sorry, Mama," explained Hannah, "when we passed that cemetery back there, I had to hold my breath."

"Why?" Mama asked, still looking at Hannah through the rearview mirror.

"Rachel told me that you have to hold your breath so you don't suck in the souls of the dead." Hannah explained, but Mama still looked confused. Hannah continued, "I was going to ask if we were almost there, but I can see the campground now!"

The park ranger at the entrance told them where their group was camped. It didn't take long at all to find the spot. As Hannah's family piled out of the car, their friends from Madison greeted them. It was then that Hannah noticed the new baby. His parents, "B" and Janie, proudly introduced him as Todd. Hannah couldn't take her eyes off the adorable baby boy with his chubby arms and legs.

Mama noticed Hannah's stare. "Todd's only seven months old, so he'll need to be around his mom and dad a lot," she cautioned.

Hannah was excited anyway. Maybe if I show B and Janie that I could be careful, they'd let

23

me push him in the stroller, she thought. Or maybe I could even feed him his dinner!

By the time Hannah snapped back into reality, Daddy had begun unloading the camping gear. He had been quick to set up the family tent and Marcy, who had never been camping, was inside, squealing happily as she bounced against the nylon walls.

"I guess the children didn't do much camping in her orphanage in Bulgaria," Mama was saying sarcastically to some of the adults. It was sad, Hannah thought. Marcy had never been to a farm, a circus...had never done a lot of the things that kids do.... Hannah almost fell through the tent door with an awkward thud in her hurry to hug her littlest sister.

After a quick roll in the tent, Hannah wandered over to the camp fire with Marcy. The parents were cooking a big spaghetti dinner. "We have that for dinner every year," Hannah said to no one in particular. She didn't really mind, though; spaghetti was one of her favorites.

"We're having corn, beans, and a salad, too," said Debbie, one of the mothers. "Everything is from our garden." Hannah helped her little sisters find plates and dinnerware, then a spot at the picnic table. Soon they were joined by most of the youngest members of the other families. Mama, as usual, was busy taking pictures. Hannah knew that one of these would be put on the refrigerator in Kansas and looked at daily until next summer.

"DO YOU NEED MORE CORN OR BEANS?" Hannah signed to Mary Pat. Marcy needed a drink, so Hannah went to the cooler to find something for all of them. She noticed chocolate candy bars in the top tray. Hmmm, she thought, I bet those are dessert. I think I'll just keep that a secret!

Hannah was right. After dinner, when the dishes were done and the sun had set, the campers toasted marshmallows for "some-mores." Hannah helped Marcy and Mary Pat put their soft, gooey marshmallows and the chocolate between the graham crackers before smooshing it all together into a little sandwich. Marcy thought it was great fun to make these little goodies, but she didn't really want to eat them. She kept handing them to Mama who would absentmindedly eat them with a sincerely signed "THANK YOU." She'll be up exercising early tomorrow, thought Hannah.

The families spent most of Saturday on the lake. One family had brought a little powerboat and another had brought a canoe. The adults were taking turns going out on the lake with groups of children. When it was time for Hannah and the little girls to go in the canoe, they all climbed in awkwardly with Debbie. Marcy liked wearing the neon life-preserver and her giggles of delight could be heard from the beach. Debbie let Mary Pat and Hannah paddle the canoe during their trip across the lake to see some water lilies and red-winged blackbirds.

As soon as they returned, one of the dads, Russ, took Hannah and her sisters out in the powerboat. They cruised quickly down to the far side of the lake. There was no beach this far down, but people could be seen fishing along the banks. The lake was quiet and peaceful and Hannah found herself daydreaming. She was startled when Russ called to her. "Would you like to help me drive the boat back?"

Hannah looked around at Marcy and Mary Pat. He must mean me! "Yes!" she said. Oh, man, she thought, my friends back home will never believe I'm doing this!

Russ showed Hannah how to turn the wheel so the boat would go where she wanted it to go. As they neared the dock, Hannah saw Mama standing on the shore, camera in hand. She waved and flashed Mama a smile that was sure to end up on the refrigerator door! Then she and Russ traded places again and he brought the boat in for a smooth docking. The children piled out. "Wow, Hannie," said Mama, "you were driving the boat! When did you learn to do a thing like that?"

Hannah felt too cool to respond to her mother. She pretended to be busy helping Marcy and Mary Pat out of the boat. "The little girls want me to take them swimming, Mama," she said in a very grown-up voice. "We're going down by the lifeguard stand." She suddenly felt older and more responsible. She was sure Mama could see it, too.

"WAS IT FUN TO DRIVE THE BOAT?" Mary Pat was asking with her signs.

"OH, YES," Hannah signed back. "AND YOU KNOW," Hannah explained as if she was a mother herself, "WHEN YOU ACT OLDER, AND ARE GOOD AND DON'T WHINE, YOU GET TO DO THINGS THAT ONLY OLDER KIDS DO. THAT'S A GOOD REASON TO BE A GOOD GIRL ON THIS TRIP."

"LIKE WHAT WILL I GET TO DO?" Mary Pat looked hopefully at her older sister.

"IF YOU ARE NICE TO MARCY AND THE OTHER KIDS ALL DAY, YOU CAN GO ROLLER SKATING WITH ME AFTER DINNER. JUST YOU AND ME WILL GO. AND IF I GO WITH YOU, MAMA WILL PROBABLY LET US GO DOWN TO THE OTHER PLAYGROUND NEAR THE RESTROOMS, OK?"

"OK!" Mary Pat was smiling again. The girls

26

ran into the water and joined the other children splashing and swimming.

That night, Hannah joined the rest of the children as they rode bikes, roller skated, and took walks around the circle of campsites. She took turns playing catch with Keith and then Kelly. Breeze stayed and talked with the adults.

As bedtime neared, the children settled down by joining their parents for some songs around the campfire. No one sang very well, so the singing lasted only until the little ones started to stretch and yawn. Not being able to hear themselves, Mary Pat and Marcy didn't sing very well, but no one seemed to mind. When Hannah stopped to listen, she realized that the hearing children didn't sing in tune, either. And then there was Todd. To the delight of the whole crowd, he squealed and clapped and interrupted almost every song.

It wasn't long before parents and sleepy children slipped off to their tents. Everyone was tired from a day of activities in the sun. Well, except Lindsey, who was four, the same age as Marcy. Hannah could hear the little girl's parents, Ward and Debbie, talking softly to her, trying to convince her to go to sleep. Hannah didn't think her parents were ever that patient with her! Finally it was quiet in the direction of Lindsey's tent; the little girl must have dropped off. Hannah fell asleep thinking about steering Russ's boat down a long river that never seemed to end.

Hannah woke Sunday to Marcy's excited signing in her face. "PANCAKE, PANCAKE, BERRY," Her antics made Hannah giggle despite the pinch in her back from sleeping in her thin sleeping bag. She had slipped off her mattress pad sometime during the night and woke up with only the hard ground beneath her.

"OK, OK, I'M COMING, MARCY," Hannah signed back. She hated to look too enthusiastic but Marcy was encouraged anyway. Luckily, she had slept with her clothes on so she didn't need to convince Marcy to give her time to get dressed.

No one will care what I look like, thought Hannah. They unzipped the tent and then rezipped it so bugs wouldn't get in. As Hannah turned to walk towards the breakfast area, she noticed that all the mothers and Breeze were just coming back from a walk. They all looked scruffy.

"Morning, Hannah," the mothers called. "Ready for breakfast?" Breeze asked.

"Uh-huh."

"Would you take Todd for a stroll after you're finished?" asked Janie, Todd's mother. "It's my turn to wash up the dishes." "Oh, yes!" Hannah shouted and ran off to eat quickly. She wanted to show Todd's parents that she was old enough to be responsible for their cute little boy. As soon as she finished her breakfast and cleaned up her eating area, she found the stroller and wheeled it over to

Todd and his dad.

"Oh, great," said B. Hannah could see that he had no idea how special this was for her. Suddenly Todd was in Hannah's arms. "Here you go," B said. "Can you put him in without help?"

Hannah looked down at the gift of the little boy in her arms. "Hi, Toddy," she cooed. The baby didn't wiggle or cry. He looked up at Hannah with his big blue eyes and...drooled! "Gosh," laughed Hannah, "even his slobber is cute!" Todd's dad smiled and together they strapped the infant into his stroller.

Hannah and Todd took a long walk. The other kids passed them on their bikes and later on skates and finally ran up to greet them and walk them back as they came around the circle on the last leg of their journey. Janie came to help Hannah lift Todd out of his stroller. "That was so nice of you, Hannie," she said. "I helped with the breakfast clean-up and even got a chance to spend some time with Amy and Lindsey. It's great that you are old enough to help with Todd."

Hannah grinned from ear to ear. She felt special, not just "one of the kids." Breeze and Hannah had been the only children in this group for many years but four years ago the other adults started to have kids of their own. Now when these parents watched Hannah helping and signing with her little sisters they were seeing her in a whole new way.

Hannah walked over to help Daddy pack the van. It was time for the family to start the long trip from Wisconsin back to Kansas. Summer and vacations were almost over. Hannah heard Mama and Daddy grumbling about the long drive home as she walked back and forth between them, carrying bags.

"When I get older, I'll help you drive, Dad," Hannah called up to her father, who was stationed on the roof of car, loading the car-top carrier. Her offer made him smile.

The phone was ringing as Breeze opened the front door in Kansas. It was Lauren, Hannah's best friend since last year in third grade. Lauren surprised Hannah with some school news. They were in the same class again for fourth grade! "Wow, that's great! Are Kristi and Emmy in...hey, who's our teacher?" Hannah knew that Lauren had been down to the school and read the grade lists posted on the front doors.

"Mrs. Sharrrtzzzer," Lauren said the word slowly. "I'm not really sure how you say it. Yeah, Kristi, Emmy, Megan...we're all in the same room. And guess what? Brandon and Tara are with us, too."

Brandon and Tara were deaf. Approximately 15 students who were deaf or hard-of-hearing attended Scarborough School, but Brandon and Tara were the only fourth graders. Hannah knew Brandon from third grade, but had only seen Tara on the play ground. "Oh, great," Hannah said back into the telephone, "I'd like to get to know Tara better; that's great that she's in our class." Suddenly Hannah panicked, "Hey, Lauren, what are you wearing the first day?"

"My jean cutoffs and this cool shirt my mom got for me...what are you wearing?"

"Boy, I don't know!" said Hannah. "Nothing that I took on vacation. I am soooo sick of the clothes I took to Violin Camp!"

"Oh, yeah," Lauren almost interrupted her. "How was your vacation - it was dull around here without you."

"Oh, real nice," Hannah said sincerely. From the other part of the house, Hannah heard Daddy calling her. "Listen, Lauren, I gotta go. I need to help my parents unpack. We brought back about twice what we took!"

Eight days later Hannah, Lauren, Kristi, Megan, Lindsay, Emmy, Brandon, Tara, and 15 other fourth graders sat in Mrs. Shartzer's classroom. The group was deciding on class rules but Hannah could hardly pay attention. Her thoughts were of Jessie in Wisconsin, Alliyson in Pennsylvania, and Rachel in Illinois. Summer vacation had come and gone too quickly. She was excited for school to begin but sad to think about summer being over for another year. Just then, Lauren tapped Hannah's desk and asked to borrow a pencil. Hannah passed back her newest and prettiest one. Fourth grade had begun.

Chapter 3

September

September was Hannah's second favorite month (her birthday month, July, was her first favorite, of course!). She liked September because the routine was still new at school and there were lots of fun things planned for every weekend. She and her family always attended Old Settlers' Days, went to the Winfield Bluegrass Festival, and took in one last Royals game before the baseball season and the month came to an end.

One Saturday morning, Hannah sat at the wooden kitchen table scanning the Olathe Daily News. Usually she read the headlines, weather, and comics, but today an article about Old Settlers' Days caught her attention. Old Settlers was a fall festival that featured a carnival, arts and crafts sales, performances, and the Sweet 16 Contest. "LOOK, MP," Hannah signed to Mary Pattie, "THERE'S GOING TO BE A SWEET LITTLE SIX C-O-N-T-E-S-T THIS YEAR FOR OLD S-E-T-T-L-E-R-S DAYS. MAYBE YOU CAN BE IN IT!"

Mary Pat was immediately interested. She loved clothes, makeup, hairstyles, and fashion. "HOW?" she asked, unable to read the article in the paper for herself. "WELL, IT SAYS HERE IN THE NEWSPAPER THAT YOU NEED TO FILL OUT THIS F-O-R-M." Hannah finger spelled this last word and then pointed to the square of newsprint in front of her.

Mary Pat snatched the form, jumped off her chair, and ran off to find Mama. The form was in the mail an hour later!

"Do you really think she can win?" Hannah asked Breeze later as the girls lay on Hannah's bed. Breeze had offered to French braid her hair. "Well," Breeze replied thoughtfully, "what can they expect from a six year old? And she is cute."

"She is cute..." Hannah agreed, turning her head so that Breeze could finish off the last of the braid. "But maybe we could ask her some questions that would be like the ones that the judges will probably ask her; let her practice some."

"Hey, H, that's a really good idea," Breeze came around from behind her and held her hand up for a "high five." She only called Hannah "H" when she was in a really good mood. "Let's think of some questions the judges will probably ask."

"Name, age, school, pet's names, favorite food, and person most admired," Hannah rattled off enthusiastically. "And let's have her wear a cute hat or something that will make her stand out a little bit." The two sisters were deep into Sweet Little Six strategy for the better part of the afternoon.

Hannah enjoyed this special time with Breeze. Usually her big sister was too busy with her friends to pay much attention to Hannah.

Hannah looked up to Breeze and felt comfortable with her. She could ask her opinion about things that she would never talk about with Mama or Daddy. And Breeze could explain perplexing things in an understandable way. She hardly ever laughed at Hannah's questions and usually when she did tease, she did it in a way that allowed Hannie to laugh a little at herself. It was great to have something like the Sweet Little Six contest that could bind the sisters together for the entire week.

Thursday night the whole family went downtown to see the contest. They had never been to this part of the Old Settlers' Days activities so they had no idea what to expect. Hannah was shocked to see about 50 little girls there, about half of them wearing a cute hat. She looked anxiously at Breeze. Her older sister just shrugged as if to say, Well, you can't be right all of the time!

Mama had asked Breeze to interpret for Mary Pat when the judges were explaining the rules and when it was Mary Pat's turn to walk on stage and be asked questions. "I'll be too nervous," Mama had whined. Hannah knew that Mama wasn't really nervous, she just wanted the sisters to share the experience, win or lose, by themselves. Mama had overheard them throughout the week as they planned and tried various outfits on Mary Pat as if she were a little human doll. Hannah was glad that Mama had purposely stayed out of their way and let them organize things themselves.

To the family's surprise they recognized one of the three judges now settling into their chairs on stage as Mr. Beaver, a hearing man who was the elementary principal at the Kansas School for the Deaf. Marcy and Mary Pat saw him a couple of times a week when they went to the school for the deaf after their school day at Scarborough had ended. When Mary Pat was called up on stage, she was directed towards Mr. Beaver, who, signing for himself, asked her five questions. He voiced her answers for those watching who couldn't understand her speech. All but one of the questions he asked had been ones predicted by Hannah and Breeze. The two sisters smiled confidently at each other. "Thank goodness all her answers made sense," Mama sighed as Mary Pattie walked off the stage. Hannah had to admit, Mary Pat had done a very nice job.

After all of the little girls had been asked questions, the judges met and then announced the winners. Mary Pat was chosen as runner-up! Breeze helped her back up on stage to receive her sash and a bouquet of flowers. Mama went to talk to the contest organizers about when and where the little "princess" was supposed to be on Saturday, the day of the parade. Daddy was busy taking pictures and explaining everything to Marcy. Only Hannah remained in the crowd, feeling a bit left out. Geez, why does she have to be so cute? Hannah lamented. I've never gotten flowers! And she gets to ride in a car with the Sweet Sixteen queen, too! Geez!

"Hey, Hannie," Dad interrupted Hannah's pout. "Want to go down the midway, grab some high-calorie dinner, and do a few rides?" It almost seemed as if Daddy could read her mind. It only took a few carnival rides and some treats and

Hannah had forgotten about being jealous of her little sister.

In fact, as the family walked along the carnival midway, Hannah began to feel proud of her. Deaf adults and friends from school congratulated Mary Pat and some of the deaf friends they met reminded the family that Mary Pat was the first deaf girl to ever enter the contest - let alone win one of the three spots in the car for the parade! Everyone promised to be there Saturday to wave to the little princess as she rode by with the Sweet Sixteen queen.

Saturday was a perfect day for a parade. At breakfast, Hannah showed Mary Pat how to wave to the people on both sides of the street and not let her bouquet of flowers fall. The whole family was excited and arrived at the parade route very early to get good seats. They had to take Mary Pat to a special location and leave her in the care of the Sweet Sixteen queen, who could not sign to her. Hannah was concerned, then relieved when Breeze offered to stay with MP until the parade actually started. The rest of the family walked the route, looking for the best spot from which to view the parade. They all saw lots of friends. Right across the street from where they settled in was a whole group of deaf adults. Mama and Daddy went over to talk with them and ask for signs for some parade words that they didn't know, like float and pooper scooper. Finally, it all started.

Several bands, dancers, and clowns passed by Hannah and her family before Dad spotted the Sweet Sixteen car. Everyone started to yell Mary Pat's name so she would see them, but Mary Pat could not hear them. They tried waving their arms and jumping, still yelling her name, but there was just too much noise and confusion to get her attention. Mama was usually the aggressive one in these situations, but she had her hands full with the video camera and could not come to Mary Pat's rescue.

Hannah could see that Mary Pat was fast approaching and still hadn't seen them waving and yelling like maniacs. She's not going to see us, Hannah thought, and then, surprising herself, she walked right out into the street and stood near the front of the slowly moving queen's car. She felt a little funny standing in the middle of the parade route without a costume. She was right in front of Mary Pat and got her attention as the little girl, taking her job seriously, waved and smiled to the crowds on either side of her.

It was obvious that being a parade princess was harder work than Hannah had imagined. Mary Pat looked tired already, but her little face lit up at the sight of her sister. "HI, MP," Hannah signed, hoping to give Mary Pat some encouragement. "LOOK," she directed. Daddy, Breeze, and Marcy were all jumping around and giving her the I-LOVE-YOU sign. Then, running backwards to keep just ahead of the car, Hannah pointed to the group of deaf adults on the other side of the street. Mary Pat waved toward them and gave them her best princess smile. It was all over in just a few seconds; Mary Pat was gone with the parade, and Hannah ran back to her family.

"Oh, Hannie," Mama looked relieved as she set down the camera, "Fast thinking, buddy. Way to go. You really helped her out! Thank you!" Hannah smiled at the praise and sat down beside Marcy to watch the rest of the parade.

At home, after the excitement was all over, everyone was exhausted. The family gathered to watch Mama's video of Mary Pat and Hannah before everyone ate a quick lunch and then split up and went separate ways to relax for the afternoon.

Hannah went to her room to spend time by herself and enjoy some privacy in her room. She lay on her bed and thought over all the feelings of the week—her happy time with Breeze, her jealousy over Mary Pat's winning the contest, and her pride in her own quick reaction at the parade.

———————————

The next morning, Hannah sat watching her friend Lydia across the Quaker meeting room. The family went to Meeting, which is what the Society of Friends call church, most Sundays in a small, old house in Kansas City. The living room had rows of benches for the small crowd of people with simple values who gathered here each week. Everyone sat quietly. Hannah knew she was supposed to be meditating; trying to listen inside herself, but it was difficult. Hannah found it hard not to think, but she sat quietly with the rest of the group, calming herself.

There was no minister or priest at the Meeting house. Friends, or Quakers as they are also called, believe that spiritual messages are available to all those who sit quietly in the silence and listen to themselves. If someone feels their message should be shared, they speak so that everyone can hear. Hannah could see that Marcy and Mary Pat were signing back and forth to each other; they seemed too young for the discipline that meditation requires. How could they hear the important messages, thought Hannah, if their eyes are closed when someone begins to speak?

Hannah's gaze returned to Lydia's face. The young woman's eyes were closed and she sat in a relaxed slump on the bench. She looked peaceful. Maybe she's fallen asleep, thought Hannah. Lydia was a doctor and was often up all night delivering a baby or sitting by the bedside of a person dying of AIDS. Once she fell asleep and almost toppled off the bench during Meeting!

Hannah watched Lydia's face for a long time, trying to decide if she was sleeping or meditating. Hannah knew that Lydia had been born into a Quaker family. Now, sitting in the quiet, Hannah thought about a younger Lydia maybe nine years old, just like Hannah. She imagined Lydia's long brown braid as two brown pigtails....

Hannah startled to a tap on her shoulder, which was the signal for children to go upstairs for First Day School. I think I did it! Hannah thought happily to herself. I think I was meditating; thinking of birthing and dying, and the good work that Lydia and her spouse Ann do. She followed the other children up the stairs to their class.

After Meeting, Daddy and Mama drove to their workout center. The little girls went to child care and Breeze and Hannah read books by the tennis court and watched tennis lessons. Hannah was surprised to see Brandon, from her class, having a tennis lesson! He was learning how to serve and swing backhand. Hannah watched his lesson, curious and concerned, because Brandon's teacher didn't know how to sign, although Brandon still seemed to understand most of what he said. Near the end of the lesson, Brandon spotted Hannah. "HELLO," he signed. Hannah signed a cheerful "HI" back and complemented him on his game.

"Hey, girl," the instructor yelled. "You sign, huh? Could you come here a minute and help me explain something to your buddy?"

"Sure!" Hannah replied. She followed the stairway down to the courts. The tennis courts seemed much bigger from down here. The instructor walked casually up to her and asked Hannah her name. Brandon followed close behind.

"Hi. My name is Bill." He reached out to shake Hannah's hand. "Could you explain to Brandon that he needs to keep his arm straighter as he follows through with his swing? I just haven't been able to show him exactly what he needs to do."

Hannah blushed as she began to interpret what Bill was saying, a skill that came naturally to her. She mouthed the words that Bill was speaking so that he could tell where she was in his explanation. They fell into a pattern of him talking directly to Brandon, then pausing so Hannah could interpret in signs. When Bill was finished, he turned to Hannah.

"Thanks a lot, Hannah. You were a big help. Do you play any tennis?"

"No," Hannah replied softly.

"I'd be happy to give you a short lesson to get you started. I owe you a favor for interpreting for me."

"Gosh, thanks," said Hannah. Bill handed her a racket and Hannah explained what was happening to Brandon, who was gathering his things to leave. He needed to change out of his sweaty clothes before his dad came to pick him up. Bill and Hannah walked to one end of the court and Bill showed her how to serve the ball and keep an even forearm swing. After about 20 minutes, Breeze called to her; "Mom and Dad are ready to go, Hannah. Be sure to say thank you."

Hannah could have died! I know how to say

"thank you," Breeze, you idiot, she wanted to scream back. I'm not a baby! But, instead, she turned to Bill and said. "Thanks a lot, Bill. I think tennis is a neat game. I really enjoyed the lesson."

"No problem," Bill replied. "I really appreciated you helping me today. If you're here again during Brandon's lesson, come right down to the court. You sign for me and I'll give you more lessons. Deal?"

Hannah excitedly told her family about the tennis lesson on the drive home. Mama had been telling her for years that someday she would be able to make money for signing. "When all your friends are working as waitresses earning minimum wage in college, you could earn your room and board by interpreting for deaf students," she had said. Mama knew hearing students who had done that at the university where she worked.

Now Hannah could see what her mom meant. Real interpreters were required to go to school to receive appropriate training. However, there were many times when someone with Hannah's level of signing ability could assist in an informal situation. Breeze had gotten a job interpreting for a sixth-grade boy on a basketball team. He was appreciative of how she would run up and down the court during the game, interpreting what the coach was yelling or what the other boys were saying to him. He could really be a part of the action. The boy's parents paid Breeze $5.00 for each game, too. I guess Mama was right, Hannah thought happily. I always wanted tennis lessons—now I can get them for free!

On Monday, Hannah couldn't wait to tell Lauren about the tennis lessons. She found her friend right before the last bell rang as they were settling in their desks. "Lauren, you were almost late...," Hannah started. "Oh, my sister couldn't find her tennis shoes this morning." Lauren said disgustedly. Rachel, Lauren's younger sister, was in Mary Pat's class.

"Well, guess what?" Hannah didn't stop to let Lauren guess. "I'm taking tennis lessons on Sunday afternoons, now."

"Wow, that's so neat. Great," Lauren said quickly, before Mrs. Shartzer could give them the "let's get to work" stare.

Hannah noticed that Brandon was watching her. She signed over to him from across the room, "I'M SO EXCITED ABOUT TENNIS. BILL IS GOING TO GIVE ME LESSONS AFTER YOU'VE FINISHED."

Brandon signed back. "MAYBE WE CAN PRACTICE TOGETHER?" His eyebrows were raised in a hopeful look. Hannah looked quickly at Mrs. Shartzer. She decided that she had time for one more quick comment.

"MAYBE. LET'S TALK AT LUNCH," Hannah signed and turned quickly back to Mrs. Shartzer. Her teacher hadn't noticed any of these exchanges but Ms. Terry was smiling at her.

Ms. Terry was the class interpreter and, of course, could understand everything Hannah had signed. She was a trained educational interpreter who had gone to college for two years to learn her trade. Hannah's signs were too fast for Mrs. Shartzer, but Ms. Terry had caught it all. Hannah could tell she hadn't minded that she and Brandon had been talking.

"Hannah," Lauren whispered to her suddenly. "Stop daydreaming and get into your group. Hurry!"

"Oops," Hannah moved quickly to her cooperative learning group. Today they were writing stories about the arctic animals that they had been studying. Hannah was assigned the role of "artist." Kristi was in her group, too. She was the "group reporter" and had to explain their efforts to the rest of the class. She was all business. "Let's get going, guys," Kristi coached. "I have to have something to report in 20 minutes." The groups settled into their work, Hannah included.

After school, Hannah waited for Breeze in the school entry. This was one of the days that Mary Pat and Marcy took a bus to the Kansas School for the Deaf to play and have dinner. Mama and Daddy thought it was important that the little girls had a chance to play with other deaf children and be with deaf adults.

Hannah enjoyed the days that Mary Pat and Marcy went to KSD because then Breeze and Hannah had some special time together. They would walk the three blocks home, talking or acting silly, and practice their violins without the little girls interrupting them. Then they'd make a fun snack.

Sometimes Hannah was jealous that her little sisters got to go to a special place like KSD. They would come home with intriguing art projects or special treats. Sometimes deaf adults with special talents, like mimes or artists, would do activities with the children or present special plays. Lately the children had been walking to the Olathe Public Library, which was only three blocks from KSD, to listen to a storyteller who used American Sign Language. Today Hannah and Breeze hurried home. When they arrived they saw that Daddy had been moving camping things and suitcases into the front room. His packing caught both girls off guard.

"Where we going, Dad?" Breeze asked as he passed them with a load.

"To Winfield, remember?" Dad was puffing.

"Tonight?" Hannah was lost. She had forgotten completely about this trip. Winfield was a small town south of Wichita in south-central Kansas. For two years the family had been going to a huge bluegrass festival there. They left right after school, and camped both Friday and Saturday nights.

There were five stages of entertainment, a midway of food booths, an arts and crafts sale, and lots and lots of music. People didn't play classical music on their violins the way Hannah and Breeze did. They fiddled! Around the campfires, late into the night, fiddling could be heard all around. That night, Hannah fell asleep listening to the music in the big family tent, with Daddy and her sisters tucked in around her. They looked like a sleepy, human, patchwork quilt.

Marcy was the first one up the next morning. She crawled into Daddy's sleeping bag and was soon joined by Mary Pat. It amazed Hannah that Daddy could sleep with the little girls curled up around him like grass snakes. Hannah pretended to sleep until she felt the morning sun cooking her side of the tent. Then she got up, stumbled past Daddy and her little sisters, and headed for the van.

"Good morning, Mama," she said as she opened the van door. Mama always slept by herself in the van; she was a very light sleeper and woke up easily when the others were coughing or turning in the night. "Shower time!"

"OK, Han," Mama answered. She had slept in her clothes and was slowly moving into an upright position. "Go get the others; wake up Breeze nicely."

Mama and Hannah both knew the routine. By now the little girls would be signing quietly with Dad and Breeze would still be sleeping. Hannah soon had everyone rounded up and the family drove out of the camping field and into town towards the YMCA, where they paid a dollar each to take a shower. By the time they were all clean and refreshed, Hannah was excited to get back to the festival and the music.

"Next stop, breakfast!" Daddy called like a conductor loading a train. They all piled in and headed for the restaurant where they always ate. Unfortunately, it seemed to Hannah that everyone else at the festival had decided to eat there, too.

"LOOK, LOOK, IT'S JOHN," Mary Pat signed to Hannah as they finally slid into a booth.

"Mama, look, it's John McCutcheon," Hannah repeated.

Hannah looked down the line of tables to where John McCutcheon sat. He was the family's favorite performer. He sang funny children's songs, as well as songs about hardworking people, and told wonderful stories in between each song. Best of all, a woman named Linda always performed with him. She interpreted the talk and the songs so that deaf people like Marcy and Mary Pat could enjoy the concerts as well. Sometimes Linda even let Hannah's family sit in the front row right below her. The first time this happened, Hannah thought that the people around them would be mad about the special privilege. But instead, people nodded approvingly as they took their seats. A man once even leaned over to tell Mama that it was great to see the family at Winfield and he was pleased that interpreting services were being provided.

As she looked over her menu, Mama encouraged the girls to walk over and say hello to the musician. Hannah was too shy, but Mary Pat jumped right up and headed over. She didn't really know John, no one in the family did, but she felt a bond, because wherever they saw him, Kansas City or Winfield, his concerts were always interpreted. Few performers bother to do that. The family always felt that John was aware of their presence in the front row and they watched for him to give the girls a special smile. Mama said he probably makes every family feel special that way.

Breeze followed Mary Pat. Normally, she wouldn't have had the courage to talk to John McCutcheon either, but she knew that since Mama and Daddy were enjoying their morning coffee, she would be needed to repeat what Mary Pat said. This was called "reverse interpreting." Daddy, Mama, and Breeze often reversed interpreted for the little girls so that people would be sure to understand their speech and feel more comfortable talking to them.

"Hi, girls," John said. "Having breakfast?"

Mary Pat missed his question and charged right into her request.

"Wa you pay 'Cu the Ca,' toooday?" she asked.

"Will you play 'Cut the Cake,' today?" Breeze repeated so he could understand Mary Pat's question. This was the birthday song that John had written and would surely perform, even without Mary Pat asking.

"Sure, just for you," John said and then signed a one-handed "I LOVE YOU" to Mary Pat. "Do you know all the words?"

"DO YOU KNOW ALL THE WORDS?" Breeze signed to Mary Pat while John waited. It was obvious that he was used to interpreters.

"Yes!" Mary Pat said clearly back, without signing. Everyone around John grinned. Geez, thought Hannah, Mary Pat has so much nerve. I wish I had the guts to walk right up to a famous person like that.

"WELL," Breeze said and signed diplomatically, "I THINK WE BETTER ORDER OUR BREAKFAST AND LET JOHN EAT HIS. SAY 'GOOD-BYE,' MARY PATTIE."

Mary Pattie dutifully waved good bye and almost fell over Marcy, who had come up behind her, as she turned around to go back to their table.

Hannah decided to be brave. She got up quickly and stepped up behind Marcy. "Hi," John said to the both of them. Marcy reached up for a hug and John gave her a quick one. It was obvious that John loved kids. He listened to them and talked often in his concerts about the interesting things that children said and did. He told lots of stories about his own kids. But Hannah could tell that right now it was time to let the guy eat. They would be seeing him on stage soon enough. She tapped Marcy and signaled her to return to their table. "See you in awhile, John."

"Boy," said Dad, "that was exciting."

"YAAA," Hannah felt excited as she finished up her breakfast. She didn't want to talk or even listen to everyone else. She just wanted to sit and think about Winfield and camping, and being with her family and talking with John McCutcheon.

The family finished breakfast and headed back to the Winfield Fairgrounds. They decided to split up and do different things before John's first concert started. Hannah went with her mom to look at the crafts. Daddy took the little girls to stand in line for the bathrooms. Breeze wanted to be on her own.

Hannah and Mama had just finished admiring some handcrafted medallions at a booth where a man was pedaling a pottery wheel when Hannah felt a tap on the shoulder. She turned to see Shiraine, an old family friend. Shiraine used to live in Kansas and had spent time with Mama here at Winfield in the past. Now Shiraine's family had moved to Minnesota and they had driven eight hours to attend the festival this year.

"HI," Hannah signed very big to indicate her delight in seeing this kind woman who had shared many family dinners and always seemed to have a special place in her heart for Hannah. "HOW' YA DOIN'?"

Shiraine, who had become deaf when she was 14 years old, signed fast but clear. Hannah had no problem understanding her. Finally Mama had to interrupt the two of them to get a hug in. "HAN-NIE," she teased, "SHIRAINE IS MY FRIEND, TOO."

Both Shiraine and Hannah laughed at Mama. Then Hannah moved out of the way so that Shiraine could see Mama's mouth and hands and they could have their own conversation. Hannah busied herself looking at the displays while the two women walked slowly behind her. She didn't really mind that they had to walk slowly to sign and read lips without tripping. She was considering buying a small gift and the slower pace gave her more time to look at the booths.

After lunch, Hannah's family walked to the Children's Concert that was led by John McCutcheon and interpreted by Linda Tilton. The

48

girls had sung and signed most of the songs as they drove from Olathe. Now they joined in with the adults and children who surrounded them, clapping, hooting, and occasionally signing John's songs. Traditionally, John sang his own Happy Birthday song, but the words to the verses were too fast for Hannah. And he always had a group of children hold up the words to a Russian song, "May There Always Be Sunshine." First he sang it in English, then in Russian, and finally he would teach the audience to sign it without using their voices.

In complete silence and concentration about 300 people would try to follow John and Linda as they sang in huge signs from the stage. Mama would always make sure that Marcy and Mary Pat turned around to see the crowd. It was an amazing sight! And it was encouraging to see an entire audience of just regular people signing. At some point, Linda would also sign "Somewhere Over the Rainbow" while John accompanied her on the Hammer Dulcimer. He never sang as she moved, but instead let the audience experience the grace and beauty of her dramatic movements and signs.

As they left the Children's Concert, Hannah

noticed that people were watching her family's discussion of what to do next. It made her feel proud to be able to talk about anything that she wanted with her little sisters, and to be able to converse with adults like Shiraine. It will be a fine day, Hannah thought, when everyone can both speak and sign. Marcy and Mary Pat could communicate with anyone then, and not just the limited number of people who now formed their world of sign language.

Hannah knew that more and more people were learning to sign. She knew that the interpreters at Scarborough School taught sign classes daily to all the students; she saw children approach her little sisters at the ballpark and city pool and be able to ask them easy questions and understand their answers, but sometimes she could see that their world was limited, too. Children frequently talked to Mary Pat and Marcy without realizing that the little girls couldn't speechread what was being said. Adults were always asking Hannah, or one of the other hearing people in her family, to interpret something because they couldn't sign it themselves. But today, as she walked away from John's concert, she was filled with optimism; this was the gift that John McCutcheon gave to her family.

The family attended several more concerts, camping in the field near the five stages of the bluegrass festival. They woke Sunday morning to eat a quick breakfast on the midway and watch the fiddling contests. Sometimes children competed and some played violins in the contest. Bluegrass! It was a fast, repetitive kind of country music and Hannah had never tried it. Her own violin lessons would begin in a week. She decided to ask Miss LaVonne to teach her a bluegrass piece. She lay back in the grass on the hill and enjoyed the happy music, the soft sounds of her family and friends around her, and the simplicity of the moment.

Daddy wanted to start home before lunch and stop for sandwiches and a break on the way, so Mama watched Mary Pat and Marcy while Hannah and Breeze helped him pack up the van. "Dad," Hannah asked as she handed him the sleeping bags, "did you play an instrument when you were my age?" Her dad tucked the bags into place and handed Hannah the travel pack of games to be put in the back seat. "Oh, yeah," he replied. "I played first chair clarinet —when your Mama's friend Mary didn't beat me out — all through high school."

Hannah had no idea what "first chair" meant. "Lauren wants to play clarinet," she offered, "but we have to wait until fifth grade to be in the band at Scarborough...." Breeze nudged her with a suitcase that needed to be handed to Daddy. Her expression clearly said, "Stop talking and pack." Everyone was a little edgy after two nights of not quite enough sleep and too much junk food.

Mama was herding the little girls into the van and helping them get games out for the ride home. Marcy had already begun making her Barbie dolls act like John and Linda. Hannah reclined in her captain's chair, thinking about fourth grade, the Royals game next weekend with Lauren and their fathers, and the homework she needed to do before tomorrow. The hum of the van tires sang in her ears and she soon drifted off to sleep.

Chapter 4

October

One day in early October Hannah got a letter from her friend Quinn, who lived in Omaha, Nebraska. Omaha was only four hours north by car from Olathe, so Hannah saw her more often than she did Rachel or Jessie. Quinn wrote to her in their secret code. Part of her letter read like this:

R zn kozmmrmt sveivzo gsrmth uli fh gl wl. Dszg'h z tllw mrtsg gl xzoo blf zmw wrhxfhh lfi kozmh?

Hannah hadn't used the code for several months, so it took her a few minutes to remember how to decode the message. She wrote out the alphabet and then wrote it backwards again beneath the letters in the message. Now her paper looked like this:

a b c d e f g h i j k l m n o p q r s t u v w x y z
z y x w v u t s r q p o n m l k j i h g f e d c b a

Quinn wanted to know Hannah's schedule so she could call on a night that Hannah would be home. She wanted to discuss Hannah's upcoming visit so Hannah could bring any clothes or props that they might need. Oh, boy, Hannah sighed when she finished the letter, Quinn always has such good ideas for fun. I wonder what she's up to this time....

Every year for several years, Mama and Hannah traveled by car to Omaha on the first Friday in October. Mama went to a conference and Hannah visited Quinn and her parents. Hannah looked forward to the drive alone with her Mama, just the two of them, with no sisters!

Quinn called during the week, not even waiting for Hannah to write back and tell her the best night to reach her. Fortunately, Hannah went to Girl Scouts on Monday and violin lessons on Saturday, so she was home on Tuesday night when Breeze screamed out that Quinn was on the telephone. She picked up the fake-Pepsi-can telephone on the desk in her room. Holding the can to her ear, she greeted Quinn.

"Hi, what's up?" said Hannah. "Sorry I didn't write you back yet."

Quinn wanted Hannah to bring black clothes for a dance routine she hoped they could create together. She was taking a class and was inspired to put a show together while Hannah was visiting. She also wanted Hannah to know that her parents purchased tickets for a children's play. But the most exciting news was about Quinn's new play loft.

Quinn's parents had recently purchased the house across the street from their own home. Quinn didn't know much about the two graduate students who lived there, but she described the garage, a building separate from the house with a large space over the ceiling—a loft! You could only get to the loft by climbing a rickety old ladder straight up to the ceiling and then pulling yourself up and into the big, bare room. The loft was unpainted and there were rafters protruding here and there, but Quinn's parents had given her permission to set up the space in any way she wanted. They let her have some old furniture and rugs and extra household things for the project, and Quinn wanted Hannah to help her arrange it all!

After they had thoroughly discussed all of the details, Hannah ended the conversation with "See you Friday!" She knew that Mama or Daddy would be yelling at her to get off the telephone in a minute anyway. They never let her talk very long, and she needed to finish her violin practicing so she could watch TV later.

"OK, then, bye," Quinn said back. Neither one of them wanted to end the call. "Have your mom bring you in time to go to the retirement home with us," Quinn reminded.

"I will, bye," said Hannah as she hung up the phone. She slid off the bed and danced a few steps over to her dresser. She was remembering Quinn's dad, David, and the retirement home. He went on Fridays to work with the older people who took his exercise class to feel good and stay in shape. Quinn had been going with her dad since she was a toddler and Hannah joined them when she was visiting. She and Quinn would follow along with the exercises and talk to the men and women as they moved and stretched with David.

Mama picked Hannah up early on Friday and they headed north to Omaha. She busied herself watching for the several signs that said "Welcome to Missouri" and the one that said "Welcome to Iowa." Hannah studied the map to figure out why they were winding in and out of Missouri and Iowa when they were really going to Nebraska. She enjoyed having Mama all to herself in the van and, best of all, they managed to get to the retirement home in time for David's class.

54

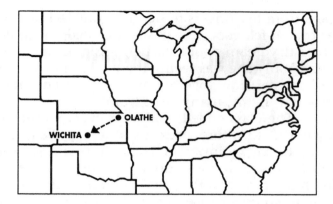

    As it turned out, the class was a good way for the two girls, who only saw each other two or three times a year, to get reacquainted. They giggled as David pulled old bike inner tubes over his head, stretching the rubber circles this way and that. Even though they hadn't been together for a while, Hannah and Quinn had no difficulty renewing their friendship.

    And David was an exercise genius! He used lots of old equipment that he recycled from around the house in various exercise routines and dances. Hannah thought he was very clever. He had been coming to the retirement home for more than ten years and you could tell that the older people cared for him as much as he liked them. He listened to their stories, humored them about their ailments, suggested ways they could move to feel more comfortable, and asked questions about their hobbies and reading. Even though Quinn's dad was a really busy person, he had made a commitment to the people in the retirement home a long time ago and he stuck to it!

    Wow, thought Hannah, he's been doing this since before I was born! She stretched her whole body, from her fingers to her toes, unwinding from the trip. It felt good, and as she stretched, she drifted into a daydream about Rachel, Jessie, Lauren, and Quinn, only she was seeing them all as much older women, dancing together in a retirement home some day, many, many years from now.

The class ended, and after everyone helped move the furniture back to where it belonged, David drove Quinn and Hannah to meet Josie, Quinn's mom, at a restaurant. Quinn had been to this restaurant so often that she asked if she and Hannah could sit together, all by themselves. "I'll help Hannah order," she shrugged casually, "and tell her what's good here." Hannah was silently thankful. Mama usually helped her decide what food to order when her family went out to eat, and she didn't want to embarrass herself here with Quinn. She listened to Quinn and her mother talk about the deli menu and when Quinn confidently listed what she was having, Hannah said enthusiastically, "Oh, that sounds so good! A hamburger with blue cheese spread, sweet potato french fries and a dill pickle! I'll have that, too!"

As the girls waited for their food to arrive, Quinn told Hannah more about the loft. "I haven't had time to do much up there. And I wanted to wait for you to come, anyway. I love to be up there. It's my own place. I can have things just the way I want them. My parents agreed that I would have to invite them up before they peeked in on their own. It really is just my place."

"That sounds so neat," Hannah agreed wistfully. She couldn't imagine such a spot at her house. Well, except Daddy once said he would build her a tree fort like they one they left back in Illinois. "Maybe this spring," he had said, without much conviction.

"Hannah, Hannah," Quinn was calling above the din of the noisy restaurant. "What should we sing for our performance?" Before Hannah could answer, Quinn jumped up and ran over to her parents' table. Hannah could see that David was giving her some change, which she immediately popped in the jukebox. "Listen to this," Quinn commanded. Hannah couldn't catch all the words to the rock-n-roll song but it was something about a motorcycle accident. There were heartfelt verses about love, dying, and being true in heaven. "Maybe you could be the boy and I could be the girl..." Quinn suggested.

Back home, Quinn and Hannah spent the better part of the evening discussing possible song selections, brainstorming dance routines, and discussing who should do what. They had a lot of good ideas, too many, really, for one weekend!

"Come on downstairs, Hannie," Quinn said suddenly. "I want to show you something." Hannah was ready for a break. She followed Quinn down the narrow back hall stairs of the house, through the kitchen, and down the basement stairs. Hannah had never seen this part of Quinn's home. The basement was old, with hanging laundry and boxes piled high against the wall, and the space had an open, friendly feel to it. Lots of sports equipment and toys were stored on shelves and in corners, and from one of these shelves Quinn pulled some big sheets of cardboard. "Our neighbor got a new refrigerator and stove," Quinn explained. "She asked if I wanted the cardboard, so I went and got it and carried it down here. It was really hard to drag it, and I had to make two trips, but I did it myself," she paused to take a breath, "and I think it will make great scenery."

Hannah nodded enthusiastically. She appreciated how hard Quinn worked to get ready for their weekend together and she could easily imagine the fun of painting the big pieces of cardboard for their performance.

"Look," Quinn continued, "my mom got us some different colors of poster paint." Hannah followed Quinn's pointing finger to the inviting, brand new jars of blue, red, green, and yellow paint that had never been touched by older or younger sisters! What fun this would be!

"And see here?" Quinn said, waving two paintbrushes in Hannah's face. Hannah could feel Quinn's excitement.

"Let's go back up to my room and figure out which acts we're going to do," Quinn suggested. "If we can get that done before we go to bed, we can start painting in the morning, after breakfast."

As the girls started up the stairs, Hannah had a very adult idea. "What my parents do when they have a list of things and can't get started...well, they rate them," Hannah started to explain. "Yeaaaaaah?" inquired Quinn, "How?"

"Like you and I could copy the list of the ideas we have for acts. Then we could each rate them with a number without talking to each other first. Then we could compare our lists and add our numbers together. The lowest numbers will be the ones we'll do." Hannah paused. "What do you think?"

"That sounds good," Quinn said as she hunted for paper and pencils. "Here," she said, "Let's see," she listed out loud, "we have the '50s number, the short jokes, the holiday song, that Broadway idea, and maybe that dance to the jazz music. That's a lot. I think maybe we could figure out three numbers and really practice them before your Mom comes Sunday morning."

"Yeah, she doesn't even know about all this and I know she'll want to get back home," Hannah said she didn't even want to think about leaving. "She's always in a hurry to get back to the girls," Hannah lamented.

Hannah and Quinn began to rate their separate lists. "Wait a minute," Quinn interjected suddenly, "is a 5 my highest favorite or the one I want least?"

"Oh, good point," said Hannah. "If the ideas with the lowest numbers are going to be the ones we do, then we need to make the one you want the most your number 1 choice. Use 1 for that and 5 for the idea you like least. OK?"

In another minute, the girls compared their lists. They looked like this:

	Hannah	Quinn
'50s number	1	2
telling jokes	3	1
holiday song	5	4
Broadway show	2	3
dance to jazz	4	5

When they added the numbers together, the '50s number had 3 points. Telling jokes had 4 points. The holiday song and dancing to jazz both had 9 points. Broadway had 5 points. "That was easy," said Quinn. "We just don't do the last two on the list. Fine...."

Hannah looked at her friend, tilting her head to one side. Quinn took jazz lessons and Hannah knew she was really excited about them. Now Hannah wasn't really sure if Quinn wanted to do the jazz number or not. "Are you sure the ones we picked are OK with you?" she asked Quinn. "Maybe we could work a few jazz steps into one of our jokes or something."

"Oh, no," said Quinn, "I gave the jazz dance a number 5 myself. It would be hard to work on that when I've been in classes for six weeks and you haven't. I think the three we picked are going to be fun. Let's get ready for bed and tell stories to each other for awhile, OK?"

The girls changed into pajamas and brushed their teeth. Josie braided Quinn's waist-length hair so it wouldn't get tangled in the night. But the girls didn't get too far with their story telling. Quinn was going to start, then Hannah would add a line, then Quinn was supposed to add another line, and so on. But the pauses got longer and longer in between their lines and soon they realized how tired they were. "It's been a long week with school, driving up here, exercising, and then all we did tonight," said Hannah slowly. "I can't really follow this story anymore. I'm just too tired."

"Me, too," said Quinn. "Let's try to sleep in really late tomorrow morning."

"Good night," sighed Hannah and the two girls drifted off to their dreams.

The next morning they were up and finished with breakfast by 9:00. "Let's design our sets," Quinn suggested eagerly. They walked over to the loft with the supplies they needed. Hannah thought the loft was a wonderful place. When the girls needed a break, they practiced their lines and moves for the different routines that were to make up the whole show. By 11:00 they were ready to paint. "Let's do it," said Quinn and the girls jumped up to retrieve the cardboard. David helped them cut the seams so they could make backgrounds for their routines that, when slightly folded back and forth, could stand alone. Then they drew, using pencil on one side for one scene, and on the back of the same piece of cardboard for another scene. They planned to turn the cardboard pieces around between their skits to create new backgrounds for their audience. By the time they got all the scenery penciled in, it was time for lunch.

"Do you girls want to take a break and go to the library after lunch?" Josie suggested.

Hannah and Quinn looked at each other. Hannah waited for Quinn to decide what they should do. Quinn looked directly into Hannah's eyes, and said, "Well..." and when Hannah nodded and smiled, she finished with "OK, Mom, thanks."

The afternoon went quickly. After the library they stopped for ice cream and then returned home to paint their scenery. It took them until dinnertime to paint all the sets to their satisfaction.

"Remember you need to save time to dress nicely for the play," Josie called to them.

"Quinn," Hannah said in amazement, "we haven't talked about the children's play! What are we going to see? Where is it?"

"We're going to the Emmy Gifford Children's Theater," Quinn explained. She went quite often so it wasn't a big deal to her but it was a special treat for Hannah. She was excited about seeing a professional play and getting ideas for their own performance.

"We're seeing The Secret Garden," Quinn added.

"Oh, I love that story," Hannah replied in a dreamy voice. "I have the book and I've seen the movie, too."

"Yeah, me, too," said Quinn, "but I like the play because it's on a stage and there aren't a lot of props and you really have to use your imagination to make the garden and the fields and the house be the way you think they should be. I like doing that."

The play was a perfect end to a wonderful day for Hannah. "Too bad it's so late," Quinn said quietly as she snuggled under her quilt. "We need to get up tomorrow and have everything ready by the time your mom gets here. Think we can do it?"

"Yeah," Hannah said slowly. "I'm packed and we're pretty organized. Let's plan on a fast breakfast, though." Quinn didn't answer. She must be asleep, Hannah thought with the last scenes of the play moving dreamily though her mind. In another minute, she was asleep, too.

Sunday morning the girls were up, dressed in their costumes, and ready for their performance long before Hannah's Mama knocked on the back door. Quinn had one of those houses where people came to the back door near as often as the front. "Mama! Hi," shouted Hannah when she saw her. "I'm so happy to see you. Good conference? Miss me?" Hannah asked so many questions her mother couldn't do much more than smile and hug her.

"I missed you, too, Hannie. Josie tells me you have a little play for us?"

Hannah was relieved to hear a happy tone in her mother's voice. She was never sure how Mama was going to react. Things that seemed like they'd be so much fun to Hannah were often the very things that Mama had no time for. Hannah had been half worried that Mama would not want to stay for the performance, not realizing that the girls had worked the whole weekend planning and practicing.

"Come sit in the living room, that's where the scenery is set up," said Josie. "I have tea and fruit waiting in there, too." "Scenery?" Mama asked. But no one was paying any attention to her ... the show was beginning!

The performance went well. The girls did their routines, changing the scenery and props with only a few mistakes. When they did goof up, they would just laugh and keep going. When the performance bobbled, the girls would look at each other, giggle, glance at their parents, and continue. Their audience smiled and nibbled on their breakfast until, all too quickly, it was all over, Hannah's luggage was in the car, and she and her mom were headed back down Highway 29 to Kansas.

As soon as Hannah walked in the door, Mama and Daddy were bugging her about putting her dirty clothes from the weekend in the laundry and unpacking her other things. "Geez, Mama," sighed Hannah. "I will, I will. In a minute. Let me relax." Hannah was trying all her old tricks to just get away from them all and keep things peaceful and unrushed. Her family was too big a change from the solitude of the car ride. Here there was the noise and confusion of her big family, everyone talking fast, hands flying, and people moving quickly from one room to another, up and down the stairs. Mary Pat started begging her to tell her about her time with Quinn, but the telephone rang and Dad yelled to her, "It's for you, Hannah. Don't talk long...."

It was Lauren. She wanted to fill Hannah in on the weekend. "Kristi came over and we talked about Halloween. She ended up spending the night. We watched a movie and had caramel popcorn. We made it ourselves in the microwave...Hannah?"

"Yeah?" Hannah said quietly. For all her fun weekend, she felt left out of Lauren and Kristi's activities.

"Did you hear what I said? You're not saying anything," said Lauren. "What's the matter?"

"Oh, I'm just tired, I guess," Hannah lied, trying to cover her feelings. "What are you and Kristi going to be for Halloween?"

"Well, we want to know if you and Emmy will be babies with us. We have some ideas for costumes and maybe we could all be, like, quintuplets!"

Hannah let out a relieved giggle. Now she was embarrassed that she thought Lauren had meant to leave her out. "Baby quadruplets?"

"Yeah, you know, we could wear sleepers like little kids wear and put our hair in ponytails and put freckles on our faces with eyebrow pencils...."

"Oh, yeah," said Hannah, "that sounds pretty good." She was thinking about the sleepers with feet that her Grandma Bette had given her for Christmas last year.

"So, how was your weekend with Quinn?" Lauren didn't really know Quinn, but she had listened to Hannah talk about her visits to Omaha often enough that she felt she did.

"Fun," said Hannah. "We spent most of the weekend working on a performance with three acts. We made up the routines and found the music and painted the scenery all by ourselves." Hannah didn't feel that her words conveyed the pleasure of it all, and instead only confirmed that it was all over for a long time. "Did you guys do much in school on Friday? What'd I miss?"

"Well, the most interesting thing was that Mr. Clark came to our class."

Hannah knew Ken Clark very well. He was a deaf man who worked at KSD. He visited Scarborough School every other Friday for a couple of hours. He tried to meet with as many of the deaf children as he could. Sometimes he talked with the siblings and friends of the deaf children and asked about their feelings or what was happening in their lives that they wanted to share with him. Hannah had talked with him several times at Scarborough School and other times at KSD when her family would go there for special events.

"He told us about how he grew up and about the first year that he went to KSD," Lauren continued. "He didn't learn to sign when he was a little boy like the kids at Scarborough do. He had to wait until he was older and changed schools to KSD. And he said he thought he might be allergic to the plastic in hearing aids—that's why he doesn't wear one."

"Were Brandon and Tara happy to see him?" Hannah asked. She imagined that they were. She had seen Tara's face light up when Mr. Clark entered their room on past Fridays.

"Oh, yeah. Sure." Lauren said matter-of-factly. "They signed so fast and they didn't use speech. None of us knew what they were all saying. I felt kind of left out watching them."

Mary Pat and Marcy had come into Hannah's room, cutting the conversation short. "Lauren, I can't hear. Sorry. The ducks are in here." Hannah said with disgust. "I need to go anyway. I have to unpack and practice violin."

"OK, Hannie," said Lauren, using the nickname that she knew was only used by Hannah's parents. "I'll see you in school tomorrow, 'K?"

"'K," said Hannah. Mary Pat was signing and talking to her as she hung up the telephone. Hannah couldn't understand what she was saying.

"WHAT ARE YOU TALKING ABOUT, MARY PAT?" Hannah said sharply. She wasn't quite ready to deal with her sisters yet. "WHAT ARE YOU SAYING...COSTUME...PRINCESS...WHAT?" The solitude of working with Quinn was already fading from her memory.

"I'M GOING TO BE A PRINCESS FOR HALLOWEEN. PINK," explained Mary Pat. "WILL YOU HELP ME FIND YOUR PINK SKIRT FROM LAST YEAR?"

"WHY?" Hannah said in honest confusion. Mary Pat was referring to the '50s poodle skirt that Rachel's mom, Robin, had sent to Hannah in the mail a year ago.

"I WANT TO PUT THAT BACKWARD FOR MY PRINCESS SKIRT. IT WILL BE LONG AND..." Mary Pat walked across the room, gesturing as to how the skirt would be long enough to touch the floor and would flow behind her.

"YOU MEAN PUT IT INSIDE...OUT—NOT BACKWARD," Hannah signed carefully. "SO THE

POODLE WON'T SHOW." Then she nodded her head as she signed the word show to reinforce that it was inside out that Mary Pat was wanting.

"YES," Mary Pat smiled, thinking that this helpful explanation meant Hannah was agreeing that she could use the skirt.

"MAYBE YOU CAN," Hannah signed, not wanting to please Mary Pat too quickly. "YOU PLAY WITH MARCY WHILE I UNPACK AND PRACTICE AND MAYBE I WILL HELP YOU LATER WITH YOUR COSTUME."

Mary Pat looked disappointed but she left Hannah's room with little Marcy trailing behind her like a puppy. Marcy doesn't even know about Halloween, thought Hannah. I'll find her a costume later, too. And with that, she started unpacking, her fun weekend truly over.

By the time she cleaned up and practiced her violin she was feeling much more positive. Hannah helped her little sisters with their costumes, using bits and pieces from the dresser in the basement play room that was filled with old clothes. Mama had saved old costumes, hats, aprons, fake noses, wigs, and other odds and ends that the girls used for make-believe. Hannah was getting too old to play with the contents of the "dress-up dresser" but on this particular Sunday evening it was fun to help the little girls explore and create their costumes!

By the time the Halloween parties started later in the month, Hannah and Mary Pat had two good costumes each! Hannah was one of the quintuplets for her school party and a cheerleader at night. Mary Pat was Snow White and Marcy was a mouse. On Halloween morning, when Mary Pat's friend, Kendal, stopped to pick her up, Mama took pictures of all of them in their costumes.

On the actual night of Halloween, the weather turned chilly and the Kansas wind was blowing a little stronger than expected. Hannah was just putting the finishing touches on her costume when the doorbell rang. The lights flashed all over the house to let the little girls know that someone was at the front door. Hannah could hear Kristi and Lauren in the front hallway. "Oh, look at the mouse and the cheerleader," they exclaimed. Then she heard their much slower speech, obviously being paired with signs, "YOU ARE A CUTE MOUSE. AND YOU ARE A VERY CUTE CHEER-LEADER."

Hannah came bounding down the stairs. The little girls do look cute, even if I get tired of hearing about it, she thought. But tonight she wouldn't have to listen to it. Mama and Daddy had promised she could go out with the rest of the quin-tuplets as long as they stayed in the neighborhood. "Hi, guys!" she called to her friends.

"Hi, baby!" Lauren called back. "Ready?"

Hannah was happy to see that Lauren and Kristi didn't want to hang around. "Let's get going, huh?" Hannah said as she maneuvered past the little girls to pick up her candy bucket and the baby rattle that completed her costume. "Byyyyyyye, Mama and Daddy,"

Hannah tumbled out through the door and into the night behind her friends. She was cold without her coat. The Kansas wind was blowing with a soft howling sound that added the perfect spooky touch to the dark night. "Happy Halloween!" Hannah shouted much louder than Mama would have ever allowed. "Happy, Happy Halloween!"

Chapter 5
November

By the time Hannie flipped the November page on the calendar that hung by her bed it was cold enough to wear a coat to school. She could still ride her bike, but the "dress season" was definitely over. Not that Hannah was big on dresses anyway; but her Mama was. "Why don't you wear that cute dress that was Breeze's," Mama might say when she woke Hannah up in the morning. Or "What about this one that Grandma Bette sent?" Hannah would always mumble something about "maybe next week," and hope Mama, perhaps distracted by Marcy, would leave her room and forget about dresses.

November. It was exactly a year ago that Mama had come home early from work one day and gathered Breeze and Hannah and Mary Pat around her. She asked if anyone had changed their mind about still wanting another sister or brother. No one had, so Mama announced that a woman had called and needed a home for a little deaf girl. She was from a country far away, but she was living in Michigan now. Hannah didn't really remember where Michigan was, but that didn't seem important as Mama continued to explain....

Mama only knew a little bit about Marcy, saying that a single woman who lived in Michigan had located Marcy and arranged to bring her to

America. The woman had decided after a week or so that Marcy was too much for her to handle. She had placed her in foster care and now social workers were trying to find a new home for her. A while back Mama had listed their family with a national adoption service, saying that they would be interested in adopting a deaf child. That's how the lady had gotten Mama's work number. After she talked with her awhile, Mama had called Daddy.

Daddy had listened to the little bit of information that Mama knew about Marcy, who was called Anna then, and then joked back, "Well, yeah, fine; I feel pregnant! Let's do it!" so Mama had come home and told the girls. Hannah remembered how excited they all were last November. As it turned out, Marcy didn't come to them until after the New Year. The girls had had about six weeks to get ready for their new sister; to tell their friends, and to let the people at Scarborough School know that another deaf student would be coming after the holiday vacation.

Nothing that exciting will be happening this year, thought Hannah. November will be a month to concentrate at school, enjoy Girl Scouts, and dream about Christmas.

Just then Breeze came in Hannah's room. "Hi, H," she said.

"Hi," returned Hannah, automatically.

"Want to hear about my birthday plans?"

Hannah figured Breeze must really be bored to want to include her in the planning of her party. But she was more than happy to oblige. Breeze was in the ninth grade, the oldest class at Indian Trail Middle School. Hannah guessed that the party would involve boys, it was a pretty exciting thought!

71

"I just want to have some kids over for pizza, I think," started Breeze. "Like, down in the basement."

"Boy kids?" Hannah asked.

"Well, yeah," Breeze said trying to sound casual. But they both knew that she had never had boys over to a party before. In fact, boys had hardly been over to the house at all. Well, not including Jared and Mike...but they were neighbors. Neighborhood boys didn't really seem to count.

"Lights on?" Hannah asked with a smile.

"Oh, right," Breeze laughed along with Hannah's joke. "We're going to sit down there and kiss and smoke cigarettes!" They both smiled sarcastically at each other.

"Won't be much for Mama to do..." Hannah noted. Mama was very big on birthday parties. She complained about planning them, that Daddy never helped, and all that. But the truth was, Mama would be really lost without all their birthday parties to plan, and Daddy could always be counted on for games and transportation and last-minute things. Mama liked to have themes, like the Jem party Hannah had when she was four, or "Smurfs," or "clowns."

"That's exactly right," Breeze agreed. "I really don't want Mama and Daddy around at all. Maybe just to meet my friends. But I don't think we'll even want a cake. I'll have to ask Amber," she mused.

This new stage in Breeze's life included checking everything she did with Amber, her girl-friend who lived three houses down their street. "Think I'll go call her," she jumped up abruptly and left Hannah staring out into the hallway.

But a minute didn't pass before Mary Pat wandered in. "WILL YOU CALL MANDY FOR ME?"

"YES, SURE," Hannah said reaching for her

Pepsi-can telephone. "WHAT SHOULD I TELL HER?"

"DADDY SAID SHE COULD COME OVER. I WANT TO KNOW IF SHE WANTS TO COME. ASK HER IF SHE CAN COME TO PLAY BARBIE'S OR WHATEVER SHE WANTS TO PLAY," Mary Pat added, trying to be polite.

Hannah dialed Mandy's number and Mandy answered. "Hi," Hannah said, "This is Hannah calling for Mary Pat." Hannah began to sign so Mary Pat could follow the conversation, too. "MARY PAT WANTS TO KNOW IF YOU CAN COME OVER AND PLAY. MAYBE BARBIE'S OR WHATEVER YOU WANT." When Mandy said yes, Hannah stopped her so she could inform Mary Pat. "Wait, let me tell Mary Pat. SHE CAN COME, MP," signed Hannah while she listened to Mandy, who had started to talk again. "OK, Mandy, I'll tell her, wait," Hannah said into the telephone.

"WHAT?" Mary Pat wanted to know.

"SHE HAS TO BE HOME BY FOUR TO GO TO KARATE."

"OH, CAN I GO?" Mary Pat blurted out, not appreciating that Hannah was still trying to keep Mandy involved in the conversation as well as interpret for Mary Pat.

Hannah didn't respond but instead spoke back into the telephone. "Mandy, wait. Mary Pat is talking to me," Hannah tried to explain. She grimaced at Mary Pat, putting her hand over the receiver and scolding her little sister, "You know you're not supposed to invite yourself to someone's house. You're supposed to wait until they invite you...."

"I KNOW," Mary Pat signed. "BUT WOULD YOU ASK HER ANYWAY, BECAUSE IF I COULD TALK ON THE TELEPHONE FOR MYSELF, I WOULD

ASK HER...."

Hannah laughed. "MANDY," she said and signed, "MARY PAT WANTS TO KNOW IF SHE CAN COME TO YOUR HOUSE LATER AND GO TO KARATE WITH YOU. COULD YOU ASK YOUR PARENTS?"

At last, when all the details were arranged, Hannah hung up. "BETTER GO WAIT BY THE FRONT DOOR WINDOW. HER MOM IS BRINGING HER RIGHT AWAY."

"I CAN HEAR THE DOOR BELL," Mary Pat retorted, but then looked guilty and quickly softened her approach. "THANK YOU FOR CALLING FOR ME," she remembered to say. She bounced out of the room and went down to the front door window to wait for Mandy's car. Hannah lay back on her bed, in mock exhaustion. She was glad she didn't have to go through all that just to talk with Kristi, Emmy, Lauren, Megan, or Lindsey. She had never tried to call Tara, she suddenly realized.

Daddy had invited Hannah to go to the airport with him to pick up Grandma Rita. She was flying in from Madison, Wisconsin, and spending the Thanksgiving holiday with the family. She came every year and every year Hannah was excited. It was a long ride to the airport, and then a long ride home again. On the way, Hannah sat in the front seat. She felt like she and her Daddy were in a bubble, the darkness outside creating a little world that included just the two of them. The bubble zoomed along the highway. Daddy talked all about his work and Hannah told him about school and friends.

Daddy parked close to the terminal and held Hannah's hand as they went in to meet Grandma's plane. Their timing was perfect because in just a few minutes there was Grandma Rita, coming down the ramp from the plane. She hugged Hannah, smelling all fresh and warm, and then Daddy, who was, of course, her son. Someday, Hannah thought as she watched them, Mama and Daddy will come and visit my family for the holidays just like Grandma does now.

On their way back home, Hannah listened to Grandma tell Daddy about her trip from Madison to Kansas, the Wisconsin football season, and about Daddy's sister, Mary Lou. Then Daddy told Grandma about the things that he had planned for her visit. Hannah liked that part. She wanted to hear about shopping, cooking, shows and restaurants! Almost as soon as they arrived home, the whole family was back in the car again, all going out for dinner. This was a very special event indeed, really setting the tone for the Thanksgiving season. Hannah's family didn't go to restaurants very often. Mama said it cost too much money and it was too hectic. But Grandma Rita always took the family to Applebees, where Hannah got a chicken dish with honey mustard dressing. In fact, when she ordered, she asked the waitress for two of the little cups of honey mustard!

Mary Pat also ordered completely for herself. Mama and Daddy had been working on this for several years now. Hannah was proud for MP that the waitress, looking along with Mary Pat at the menu, could follow her spoken requests. When it was Marcy's turn, Mama pulled out a wrinkled paper menu that she kept in her purse. It had a picture of each basic food that a young child might order, the name of the food, and a sign. Marcy pointed to the picture of the spaghetti on the little menu and signed to the waitress, "I WANT SPAGHETTI AND COKE." Mama reverse interpreted for her, telling the waitress what Marcy was signing. The waitress nodded and smiled in acknowledgment. There were many deaf people who came to the Applebees restaurant in Olathe.

After dinner, the group headed home to relax and watch TV before bed. Hannah listened while Daddy explained the television captioner to Grandma. "See," he said, "it puts a sentence on the screen so Mary Pat knows what is being said."

"Why isn't that on my television?" Grandma Rita wanted to know.

"You have to have a television that will transmit the captions," Daddy explained. "Older TVs don't have the captioning computer chip in them."

"Does Mary Pat really read it?" Grandma asked.

Hannah didn't think Mary Pat could read the captions - sometimes even she had trouble. The words flash up very quickly and sometimes it was hard to know which character was talking. Sometimes the words appear as a string of weird symbols because the captioner didn't "catch" the conversation. But that usually happened during "live" shows, like the news, and Mary Pat didn't watch that kind much.

Before long, everyone was yawning and began drifting off to bed. Grandma was staying in Hannah's room, so Hannah was sleeping with Breeze.

When Hannah woke on Thanksgiving Day, she could already detect delightful smells coming from the kitchen downstairs. Grandma Rita's cooking! she smiled to herself as she put on her robe and slippers. No need to hurry getting dressed today! Hannah decided to be really lazy and didn't even comb her hair before she went downstairs.

"Watcha makin', Grandma?" Hannah called out happily as she rounded the kitchen corner.

"Cranberries," Grandma Rita said. "And then you can help me bake the pie."

Hannah always made the pie, every Thanksgiving. She was pleased that Grandma remembered.

She moved through her breakfast routine at a much slower pace than usual, savoring the smells from Grandma Rita's cooking and enjoying the lack of schedule. Mama had obviously given over the kitchen to Grandma, and having set the dining room table with all the good placemats, glasses, and plates, she relegated herself as "go fer." "What's a 'go fer'?" Hannah asked.

"I'm the person who 'goes for' things - like running up to the grocery store and getting the special things Grandma needs," Mama laughed.

Hannah read the comics, ate a bowl of cereal, picked a CD of music for the listening pleasure of the kitchen crew, and sat down to draw with Marcy. Her sisters had an art table in the kitchen where Mama and Daddy kept a constant supply of crayons, paper, glue, scissors, and drawing books. The little girls spent lots of time there every day and Hannah often enjoyed helping them create their master-pieces. Mary Pat especially liked to "do projects" and "experiments." She would bring home library books and attempt to duplicate the ideas they outlined. More than once Mama had waited a few days and then quietly thrown away some science concoction after Mary Pat had forgotten all about it. Helping the little girls with their artwork and projects gave

Hannah the excuse she needed to scribble, construct, and mix odd combinations of food or things found outside. Today she simply colored with Marcy, listening to the comforting family sounds and smelling Thanksgiving.

Daddy had brought home a new computer game for Hannah and when she tired of coloring she wandered over to it. The computer station was near the kitchen, so Hannah was able to work on the program while still being close to the action. "Hannah," Dad said just after she had sat down at the computer, "you need to get out of your PJs, make your bed, clean up your room, and practice violin."

"Oh, Daddy..." whined Hannah. She and Daddy both knew it was a fake response. This was an often repeated ritual. It wasn't as if Hannah didn't know the morning routine by now. It had been "the rule" for most of her life: get dressed, clean your room (making your bed and throwing your dirty clothes down the laundry shute), and fix your hair BEFORE coming down for breakfast. She had gotten away with breakfast first today because it was a holiday. Now, Dad had caught up with her. "Bet you thought you could stay in those pajamas all day, huh?" Daddy teased back.

Hannah did as she was asked. She learned long ago that it was either "go willing" or go with a parent hot on her heels. She preferred to go alone and still have some control over the pace of her morning. It really didn't take her long to clean up her room, and practicing took her mind off Thanksgiving. Well, at least for awhile. An hour after she had entered, she exited her bedroom and headed back down to the kitchen.

"Want to make your pie?" Mama asked as

Hannah rounded the corner into the kitchen for the second time that morning.

"Yup!" Hannah replied. Hannah had made a Thanksgiving pie for the family meal for at least three years. She was sure she could do it by herself this year.

"OK, here's your space," Mama said, pointing to the corner of the kitchen counter. It was a good spot for the project. Under this section of the counter were all the bowls and measuring cups and the mixer. Hannah reviewed the recipe for pumpkin pie and began to gather her supplies. She was glad that Mama was preoccupied helping the little girls decide what to wear for dinner.

"How many eggs do you need, Hannie?" asked Grandma Rita.

"One," Hannah replied with confidence. She didn't want any help baking this year but she didn't want to hurt Grandma's feelings either.

Fortunately, Grandma was busy with the turkey. She and Daddy were stuffing and tying it up with string. They were laughing and telling stories about past Thanksgivings as they worked.

"CAN I HELP YOU MIX THE PUMPKIN PIE?" Mary Pat asked Hannah, appearing suddenly from the doorway off the dining room.

"ONLY FOR A FEW MINUTES," Hannah had learned that MP had a short attention span and letting her help with one or two things satisfied the little girl. If she said no, which is what she really wanted to say, Mary Pat would just bother and bother her and sooner or later she would complain to Mama. Then Mama would try to make Hannah feel guilty by asking why she just couldn't let her sister do one small thing......

Mary Pat had helped for only a minute when she was called away by Mama. "I WANT YOU TO

HELP ME MAKE BREAD THIS YEAR," Mama told her. Mary Pat's fact brightened considerably. "GREAT!" she signed back and moved to another part of the kitchen to be with Mama.

The afternoon progressed, everyone going in and out of the kitchen area often. Mama did puzzles with the little girls, Breeze talked with Grandma about her school activities, Grandma showed Hannah pictures from a trip she had taken to Europe, Daddy played cards with his mom. Grandma even had time to finish the New York Times crossword puzzle! The telephone rang with greetings from relatives and friends. Everyone put on nice clothes.

Finally it was time to be seated at the table. Breeze lit the candles in Great Grandma Byrnes' candle holders, Mama poured the water in the tallest glasses while Daddy poured apple juice into the smaller ones, and everyone sat down. Hannah looked down at the table before her. She felt both lucky and happy. It was a beautiful meal and for a minute no one wanted to disturb the perfect dishes of cranberry sauce, bread, sweet potatoes, mashed potatoes, or platters of light and dark turkey meat. The pumpkin pie that Hannah had made was cooling on a rack in the kitchen, its warm smell mingling with the Thanksgiving smell of the turkey and gravy.

"Eat slowly," Daddy advised. And Hannah did. She tried to stretch out the dinner, mentally capturing her parents, her sisters, and her Grandma in her mind. I love Thanksgiving, she thought. I want to remember this Thanksgiving when I'm as old as Mama and Daddy.

Chapter 6

December

*H*annah was ready for Christmas! She was old enough to have earned and saved money for some gifts and she was making others. In the last couple of years, as she had gotten older and understood more about giving presents, she had sometimes felt uneasy about the quality of the gifts she made or chose. But not this year! This year she was secure in her ideas and almost giggled out loud as she imagined her family members and friends opening the packages from her.

Even the weather was cooperating. Snow had floated down several times and a thin but presentable blanket of white covered the lawns with only a few stubborn blades of grass still poking up in the fields beside Hannah's home.

Hannah hadn't seen much snow since they moved to Kansas —winters here were mainly made up of cold days with an occasional ice storm. The little girls didn't even wear their rubber boots much and Hannah, being too old now for the brightly colored galoshes, was secretly pleased to be allowed to just wear her "hard" shoes, as Mama called them, during the winter season.

But this year there was plenty of snow! Morning after morning the hearing aid in Mary Pat's right ear whistled as she pulled her stocking hat down over her head, preparing for school. Mary Pat wore a special piece of hearing equipment, called a cochlear implant, on her other ear. The implant was very expensive. Both she and Marcy had had cochlear implant surgery and now wore tiny microphones attached on an ear mold on their left ears. These microphones absolutely could not get wet, and Mama seemed to think it was Breeze and Hannah's mission in life to make sure they didn't! It wasn't such a problem in the morning, because Mama drove them all to school, but after school, when the girls walked home with Hannah or Breeze, they needed to be able to hear in order to cross the street safely. Mama was always reminding Hannah and Breeze that the stuff the little girls wore had cost thousands of dollars. All of the girls endured lots of morning discussion about the equipment on the days it snowed.

This past week, Hannah had been feeling the pressure! Both MP and Marcy were stubborn AND smart. Hannah knew that the girls would not allow her any control over them, and that included listening to their older sister on the way home! She tried to explain this to Mama and Daddy, who nonetheless expected her to get the little girls home with dry ears and aids. But Hannah wasn't thinking much about all that today.

It was Saturday and it was snowing! Hannah had shoveled the driveway two or three times already this winter and she was getting ready to do it again. The older girls would hurry home from school to try to surprise their parents with a clean driveway. Daddy came home first, relieved, Hannah was sure, to see them almost finished with a task that would have fallen to him. Hannah really enjoyed being outside and shoveling with Breeze. Today she and Breeze had lots of time; they were not planning on rushing the job.

Hannah fished around the umbrellas, balls, and roller skates in the front hall closet, looking for first one boot and then the other. Breeze was already outside, clearing neat rows of snow from the driveway with Daddy's big shovel. Patch, their dog, was prancing behind, blowing the snow with his snout like a sheep dog vacuum cleaner. He acted like he loved the snow as much as Hannah did.

The girls worked hard to clear the snow down to the end of the driveway. They had allowed the light flurries that fell on the cleared walk behind them to settle, creating a pretty, light layer over the gray cement. At the end of the driveway the snow was deep and wet, and they stood for a moment looking at it, uncertain how to begin chipping into the hard thick row left by the snowplow earlier that morning.

Just then Mama called from the house. She must have been watching them to have timed her request so perfectly. "You girls come on in now and get some hot cocoa. I'll finish up."

As Hannah and Breeze put their shovels up against the garage and headed to the front door, Mama was just coming out of it. "I'll finish up the end," she repeated. "The snowplow makes it so hard to shovel through that high ridge of snow there."

"Great," Hannah sighed thankfully as they passed.

"Good plan," Breeze teased. "Good plan," was what Mama said when one of the girls managed to come up with what Mama had wanted them to do all along. Mama laughed to hear her words thrown back at her.

"Watch Mary Pattie and Marcy for me while I'm outside and make sure they don't get into trouble. They can watch TV if you want. Hannah, will you put the star on the tree? Breeze, you lay the skirt underneath, OK?"

Hannah and Breeze smiled at each other and trudged into the house. Hannah looked at the Christmas tree, standing in its corner, bare and ready to be decorated. "This is going to be a great Christmas," she said softly to Breeze, and headed for the kitchen and the cup of hot cocoa that Mama had fixed just for her.

Hannah watched as Marcy's classmates and their parents signed the "Happy Birthday" song. She and Mary Pat had made the little girl's cake and Marcy was loving all the attention. Hannah felt warm and happy for her, too. Marcy deserved to have a hundred more nice parties!

Mama had been so impressed with how independently Hannah made Marcy's birthday cake, she asked if Breeze and Hannah would make some Christmas cookies. The girls decided that the following Sunday afternoon would be the best time. They used sugar cookie dough from the grocery store, rolling it out on the kitchen table. Mama had taken Marcy and Mary Pat out shopping so they wouldn't get in the way. Dad was in the basement watching a football game on television while he did schoolwork.

"Want to make blue frosting?" Breeze asked mischievously.

Hannah laughed. She knew that Mama would not be expecting blue frosting on the cookie candy canes they were making, but she was ready for a change in tradition! "Sure," she replied without hesitation. "This is going to be a great Christmas!"

It didn't turn out to be the Christmas that Hannah expected at all. One morning later that week, Hannah woke, ready for a day of school as usual. She was surprised to see that it was just 6:30 by her clock. She could hear Mary Pat and Marcy already downstairs in the kitchen.

Mama would probably yell at her if she didn't

get dressed and fix her hair before going downstairs but her curiosity got the best of her, and she started down the stairs anyway. Just then, surprisingly, Mama came in the front door! Mama was wearing sweats and her hair was very messy. She was surprised to see Hannah, too. "Hi, Hannie," Mama said slowly.

"Good morning, Mama," Hannah said back. She tilted her head to one side, trying to think where Mama could have been already.

"Come sit on the daybed," Mama said, without even taking off her coat, "I want to tell you about something." By now Hannah was really curious and really worried.

Just then Lynn Hayes, who worked with Mama up in Kansas City, came around the corner with Mary Pat and Marcy. Something very odd was happening. It was a Thursday... it was 6:30 in the morning ... Lynn was here. "Mama," Hannah said softly, "what's wrong?"

Mama waited until all the children were seated around her on the floor in front of the daybed. Then she began to sign slowly, using simple language so Hannah's little sisters could understand. "DADDY IS IN THE HOSPITAL. HE IS SLEEPING RIGHT NOW." Even though Mama tried to start her explanation on a positive note, Mary Pat burst into tears. Mama reached down and patted her shoulder, trying to both comfort her and get her to look up again. "LAST NIGHT HE WAS DRIVING HOME FROM HIS COLLEGE CLASS AND HE HIT A TRAIN."

"A train?!" Hannah blurted out in disbelief. She could hardly comprehend what Mama was saying and the worst pictures she had seen on television flooded her mind. She wanted Mama to say more and not say anything else, all at the same time.

"Well," Mama started again, not seeming like she wanted to continue. "THIS HAPPENED LATE AT NIGHT, AFTER YOU WERE ALL IN BED. I WOKE UP BREEZE AND TOLD HER, THEN CALLED LYNN TO COME OVER AND BE HERE, AND THEN I WENT TO THE HOSPITAL TO BE WITH DADDY."

"WHO CALLED AND TOLD YOU?" Hannah wanted to know.

"A POLICEMAN CALLED AROUND TEN. HE SAID DADDY WAS IN A BAD ACCIDENT AND WAS IN THE OLATHE HOSPITAL. SO THAT'S WHERE I WENT."

"IS HE THERE NOW?" asked Mary Pat.

"NO, HE HAD TO HAVE SURGERY ON HIS ELBOW AND SO THEY TOOK HIM IN AN AMBU-LANCE UP TO THE MEDICAL CENTER. YOU KNOW, WHERE I WORK...?"

"WHAT HAPPENED TO HIM?" This time it was Breeze.

"HE HAS A BROKEN ELBOW ON ONE SIDE, SOMETHING IS BROKEN IN HIS HIP, BUT THEY ARE NOT SURE YET EXACTLY WHAT. HIS NOSE IS BROKEN, TOO." She stopped. It was enough for the girls to figure out that their Daddy was seriously hurt.

"WHAT HAPPEN TO THE VAN?" Hannah asked suddenly. But she knew the answer.

"THE VAN IS GONE, HONEY," Mama said, shaking her head in disbelief herself.

There was a chorus of groans.

"AND CHRISTMAS?" Mary Pat began, but then just stared at her Mama, waiting for a miracle.

"WELL, DADDY WON'T BE HOME FOR CHRISTMAS. THAT'S JUST TWO WEEKS AWAY AND HE HAS A LOT OF BROKEN BONES. HE'LL HAVE

TO STAY IN THE HOSPITAL FOR A FEW WEEKS."

Just then the telephone rang. Hannah sighed in relief. She didn't want to hear any more. All the girls were sniffling and hugging each other. Lynn answered the telephone, and was bringing it to Mama. "It's a neighbor," she said.

Mama took the telephone slowly. It was as if she was afraid of who it was and what they might say. "Yes, he was," Hannah heard her say. Then Mama walked to the door, continuing to talk quietly on the portable telephone. Mama opened the front door and picked up the newspaper. She walked to the kitchen, away from the group of crying children in the daybed room. "Oh, no," Hannah heard her say from the kitchen. "It's the front page story."

The girls all hurried into the kitchen. Mama had spread the newspaper out on the counter.

"WHAT, WHAT?" Mary Pat was saying. She couldn't hear Mama from the kitchen and didn't understand why everyone had moved so quickly.

Mama ignored her. "WHEN YOU SEE THIS, I WANT YOU TO REMEMBER THAT YOUR DADDY IS ALIVE AND IS GOING TO BE OK," Mama said in a very serious tone of voice. Then she moved aside and showed them the Olathe Daily News. There was a large black and white picture of a smashed up van that Hannah didn't even recognize. She seemed to be thinking like she did after a sleep-over when she hadn't gotten enough sleep. "IS THAT OUR VAN, MAMA?" she almost whispered, forming her signs in soft, slow handshapes.

The little girls were watching their Mama carefully. When they saw her nod they both burst into tears again. Marcy started signing, over and over, "MY DADDY ACCIDENT TRAIN...SORRY."

She let Lynn take her upstairs.

"I WANT YOU ALL TO GO GET DRESSED NOW," Mama said as Lynn and Marcy left the room. Mary Pat obeyed quickly but Hannah stayed behind.

"Mama, I don't really want to go to school today," Hannah said, making it a question. She guessed that everyone at school would be talking about the accident and she wasn't sure she wanted to be there.

"I know, honey," said Mama. "But I have been up all night. Lynn, too. I need your help today. I need you kids to all go to school so I can get some sleep, call my brothers, and think what we are going to do next."

Hannah still stayed.

"Tell you what," Mama said suddenly. "What if I promise I will take you to see Daddy after school?"

"OK," Hannah agreed. She wanted to help Mama, and she wanted to see for herself that her Daddy was going to be OK. "Will you come early? Get us from school early?"

"Well, I can't really promise that. I don't know what I'll have to do today. But I'll drive you to school this morning and I'll come in and explain everything to your teachers. I'll tell them that if you can't make it through the day that you can call. I'll come and get you from school if you really can't make it—and if I'm here."

"Are you sure, Mama?" Breeze spoke up now. "I could stay home and help, you know." She looked hopeful, not wanting to go to school either.

"No, I need you guys to go to school today," Mama said in a tone of voice that ended the discussion. Hannah and Breeze turned toward the stairs and their rooms. Hannah felt Breeze's hand slip into hers, and they held hands all the way up the stairs.

Mama did take them to school. Hannah thought that she was hoping that they wouldn't be noticed by anyone in the school entryway so she could make the rounds of the girl's teachers and get back home. Mama was shy in some ways, Hannah knew. Shy like Hannah herself.

But when their little group pushed open the heavy front door to the school, Hannah saw many adults clustered near the office. They had seen the newspaper and rushed over to comfort the family. Everyone was hugging everyone, and Hannah felt the arm of Mr. Cox, the principal, wrap around her shoulders.

"What happened?" "Is he OK?" "Where is he now?" When Mama started to explain it all again, Hannah turned away. She couldn't stand to hear the story again. Not yet.

"I need to talk with their teachers," Mama said as if apologizing, and they moved down the hall towards Marcy's classroom. After talking with her teacher, Miss Nettie, they went on to Mary Pat's teacher, Mrs. Stryker, and finally, Hannah's. "Oh, hi," Mrs. Shartzer said casually when she saw them. But when Mama didn't answer and Mrs. Shartzer looked more carefully at Hannah's tearstained face, she stopped what she was doing. "What's wrong? What happened?"

"Did you see the paper—the Olathe Daily News—this morning?" Mama started. Hannah walked over to her desk and Breeze followed her. Mama finished talking with Mrs. Shartzer, gave Hannah a quick hug goodbye, and left. Hannah was glad no one else had come into the room yet. Her classmates were all still in the gym, waiting for the first bell to ring. Tears started in her eyes, but she held them back.

"See you after school, baby...OK?" Mama asked. She needed Hannah's permission to leave as much as Hannah needed to believe that Mama would bring better news by the time school would be over.

Right before 3:00, Hannah was called to the office. Mrs. Stryker and Ms. Hatcher, the speech teacher, greeted her. "Hi, Hannah," they said kindly. "We have something here for your family. And your mother called; she'll be here in a minute to get you kids."

There were several bags of groceries on the table behind the women. "Dinner?" she asked.

"Yes." said Mrs. Stryker. "There should be enough for several meals. Then your mom won't have to worry about cooking for a few days. Do you kids like spaghetti, pizza, and chocolate cake?"

"Yes...thank you," Hannah said. The words didn't even sound like they were coming from her. Mama would have wanted her to thank them just like she was doing, but she hadn't even thought about food all day and couldn't imagine eating!

When Mama came to pick the girls up after school, Breeze was already with her. Mama was surprised to see the sacks of groceries. "How kind of you all," she said as she looked from the women gathered around the table back to the bags. "I, I hadn't even thought about feeding us...it's been a very strange day." But as soon as Marcy and Mary Pat came from their classrooms to join them, she forced a smile, and handed each of the girls one of the bags. "CAN EACH OF YOU GIRLS TAKE A BAG AND CARRY IT TO THE TRUNK?" she said, handing something to each.

They were all very quiet as they loaded Mama's little compact car. Hannah tried hard to make this day less odd by creating her usual after-school conversations in her mind. She thought about their normal fights about who got to sit in front, their teasing about which boys chased her sisters at recess, and their usual discussion about after-school snacks. But today none of that mattered. She leaned back into the seat and hugged Marcy, who was smashed in beside her.

When Mama started talking quietly with Breeze, who was sitting in front, Hannah leaned forward to hear, too. She began to interpret for Mary Pat. Marcy didn't ask where they were going or have any other questions, so Hannah just let her be. She's too little to really understand anyway, she thought.

Mama was telling Breeze that they needed to get Daddy's backpack from the van and that the police had called and had his wallet. Then they could go see him in the hospital in Kansas City. Mama turned to Hannah in the back seat as she explained this last sentence. She saw that Hannah was telling Mary Pat about their plan. "Thanks for interpreting, Hannah," Mama said with sincerity. Hannah just smiled back. They all needed to be good and try to help Mama now. She knew that if she were MP she wouldn't want to miss anything. The girls were all curious and worried and hopeful all at the same time.

Mama pulled into a parking lot of towed cars not far from the school. When Hannah saw the van, she couldn't even get out of the car with the others. Their pretty van was smashed in on all sides, but especially on the driver's side. It was covered with mud, and the front tires were missing. Mama and Breeze walked like robots towards it and tried to reach in through the broken windows to retrieve anything they could. The little girls just stood and stared. None of them was able to comprehend that this was the same van that had carried them in such style from state to state in the warm sunshine of last summer. Hannah suddenly felt very cold.

A quick stop at the police station to get Dad's wallet and they were on their way to the University of Kansas Medical Center. It usually took about 30 minutes to get to the hospital where Mama worked, but today it seemed to take hours. When they finally arrived, parked, and rode the elevator to the fifth floor, Hannah started to really worry. What would Daddy look like? Was he able to talk? She hadn't asked Mama these questions and no one had offered much specific information. Daddy's room was located right beside the nurses' station. Hannah didn't think that was a very good sign. He's probably really serious if he's in a room so close to them, she thought. All of the nurses and orderlies watched the girls file into Daddy's room, ever so quietly following Mama.

Daddy might not have looked quite so awful if he hadn't been so surrounded by white. White sheets, a white sling on his casted arm, white blankets draped over the end of the bed, white bed clothes. Daddy's head was red and swollen and bruised. He didn't look like himself at all. His nose was twisted in a weird position. Mama had said it was broken, right? Hannah couldn't remember.

Hannah was glad Daddy was sleeping and couldn't see them as they all stood around his bed and stared. No one said a word, and Mary Pat and Marcy started to cry. "Kent, Kent," Mama sang to

93

Daddy softly. "Your girls are here. Can you wake up and say hi?" Hannah hadn't ever seen Mama talk to Daddy so sweetly. It worried her even more. What if he couldn't wake up to see them? Hadn't he just had surgery on that elbow? Hannah tried again to remember what Mama said about all of his injuries.

Daddy turned his head slowly to the sound of Mama's voice. His eyes were still closed but a smile spread painfully across his face. "Hi, girls," Daddy said. As soon as Mama began to interpret, the little girls stopped crying and turned to watch his mouth. Mama moved carefully around to the other side of the bed so that they could watch both Daddy talking and her signing at the same time. "I won't be signing for awhile, MP," Daddy said apologetically. Mama, who was standing behind his bed, out of his sight line, touched his shoulder. He turned his head towards her. Every move he made was done very slowly and carefully. "Let me explain your injuries to them so they understand; you rest a minute." Daddy didn't argue with Mama, he just closed his eyes. For all the times Hannah had hated to hear her parents arguing, she would have loved to hear Daddy say something like, "No, no, I can tell them myself." But he closed his eyes and let Mama talk. One elbow was broken and the other had been caught under the van and had nerve damage. He wouldn't be able to use them or to sign for several weeks.

Too soon for Hannah, a nurse came in and motioned to Mama. "Time to go," Mama said to the girls, and for once no one argued with her. It all seemed very unreal to Hannah. She just wanted to be home, in her own room, with all of her family in the same house.

When Hannah woke the next day, it was Friday. She was glad there was only one day before the weekend to face the questions that all her friends were asking and for which she had no answers. The teachers at Scarborough were giving her lots of special attention, but it seemed to Hannah that Lauren, Kristi, and Emmy were angry with her because of it. Hannah knew in her heart that really couldn't be so, but she noticed them whispering to each other and they stayed away from her at recess. Mama said they were just little girls and didn't know what to say to her. Hannah thought that was probably true because she didn't know what to say to them, either. She wished, not for the last time, that Daddy had never run into that train.

Mama took them to see Daddy again after school. Already he looked much better. His bruises were fading and he was more alert. They still couldn't stay with him very long, and when they arrived back home Uncle Artie, Mama's brother, was waiting at the house to greet them. What an unexpected surprise! He had flown from Madison, rented a car, and found the house. "Hi, Hannah," he had said when she first saw him, "Jessie says hi to you and sends a big hug."

Uncle Artie had never visited them before, but he settled himself right in. He was a bundle of energy, walking around the house, offering to fix this or call here or do that. Hannah was glad that Uncle Artie didn't talk about Daddy or the hospital. All Mama had done for two days when she was home was talk on the telephone. As soon as she would tell the whole horrible story to one person, someone else would call. Hannah got so she would just leave the room when she heard the phone ring.

But tonight the telephone was quiet. There had been a second story about the accident in the newspaper that day that talked about the lack of signals on the road at the train crossing.

"Want to call Jess?" Mama suggested to Hannah. "You could thank her for sending her Daddy to help us. She probably wishes he were home right now to help her with her holiday shopping."

Hannah got the portable phone from the kitchen.

"Thanks, Mama," she said as she passed the dining room where Mama and Uncle Artie were talking. She dialed and was glad when Jessie answered the telephone. The two cousins talked for a long while and this time, no one told Hannah to get off the phone.

"Want to go ice skating tomorrow?" Uncle Artie asked as Hannah was hugging him good night. Hannah turned to interpret his question to the little girls, who were behind her waiting for their turn to give him a kiss before bed. Marcy and Mary Pat jumped up and down with delight. Hannah smiled too, but she was skeptical. "Don't you want to go and see Daddy?" she asked, thinking that surely most of the day would be spent at the hospital.

"Well, your Mama and I will visit your Daddy in the morning, but we need to have some fun around here, too! I want to take you skating and to a restaurant called Fuddruckers. I looked in the phone book while I was waiting for my luggage at the airport and you have one here in Kansas City...."

"F-U-D-D-R-U-C-K-E-R-S?" Hannah asked with a puzzled face as she fingerspelled the funny word for her sisters.

"Yeah, your cousin Trevor always goes there with his hockey team. It's a neat place."

Hannah woke on Saturday well rested and feeling better than she had the past two days. While Uncle Artie and Mama were at the hospital, she and Breeze did their usual Saturday morning chores. Then she practiced her violin. It felt soothing to be back in a familiar routine. Her music brought her some comfort, too.

That afternoon, Uncle Artie did take them ice skating. It surprised everyone that they were exhausted after being on the ice for just an hour. Mama and Uncle Art had tried to help Marcy, who of course had never skated before. She was like the fawn in the Bambi story, slipping and thumping on her knees, smiling and trying again and again to stand upright. Towards the end, when the children were changing back into their street shoes, Mama surprised them by doing a few fast laps, zooming around the rink weaving in and out of the skaters. "Exercise," she panted, when she had rejoined them. "It feels great to get some exercise." Breeze nudged Hannah next to her.

On to Fuddruckers Restaurant. What a fun

time! Relaxing, eating the good hamburgers, listening to music, and joking with Uncle Artie. Breeze told him about how the family had planned to go to Florida for vacation in just a few days to visit Grandma and Grandpa Luetke, who were Mama and Uncle Artie's parents. Then they were to drive across Florida to see Daddy's sister and her family. Grandma Rita was with them now for a couple of months — she went every winter. Anyway, Hannah thought, now Daddy was in the hospital, the van was a wreck, Christmas was a week away, and there would be no vacation in Florida.

Mama had been listening and watching the girls. "YOU KNOW," she began, "WHEN DADDY COMES HOME FROM THE HOSPITAL, HE WON'T HAVE ANY CASTS ON. THEY TOLD US TODAY. HE'LL HAVE TO BE IN A HOSPITAL BED, PROBABLY IN THE LIVING ROOM, AND WE'LL HAVE TO BE VERY CAREFUL WHEN WE ARE AROUND HIM. IF ONE OF YOU FALLS INTO HIM, WITHOUT CASTS TO PROTECT HIS ELBOW AND HIP..." Mama paused.

"I MADE A DECISION TODAY THAT I HOPE YOU WILL LIKE," she continued. Breeze, Hannah, and Mary Pat looked up from their food. Marcy was busy watching some other customers fooling around at a nearby table and wouldn't have understood Mama's complex language anyway. "IF I BOUGHT TICKETS FOR YOU TO FLY TO FLORIDA, WOULD YOU BE GOOD AND GO, AND STICK TOGETHER, AND HAVE A FUN TIME?" Hannah laughed. Maybe Mama was rambling because she had been worried that the girls wouldn't go by themselves. But now Mama laughed too as Breeze nodded vigorously, Hannah clapped her hands, and Mary Pat jumped up and down in her chair. "Yes, YES, YES," they all cried out together. "We want to go!"

Uncle Artie left the next day, but not before convincing Mama that the girls should be allowed to open one Christmas present each. It was only a few days early. After he left, Mama made the arrangements for the girls to go to Florida. This time Hannah didn't mind all the telephone calling. They would have to change planes in Dallas, Texas. Mary Pat had a half-sister there and her parents would help them get on the right plane. Then Grandma and Grandpa Luetke would meet them at the airport in Florida. They would spend a few days in Naples, on the west coast, and then Grandpa would drive them over to Ft. Lauderdale and Aunt Mary Lou's family, on the east coast. Their aunt and uncle were going to rent a van to take the girls to the beach and the movies, as well as other adventures involving, Hannah hoped, alligators and wild birds and other tropical animals. They would be with their cousins, Bradley and Justin, whom they had not seen for three years, and Grandma Rita was going to be there, too, baking cookies, and helping with all the activities. It sounded like a dream to Hannah.

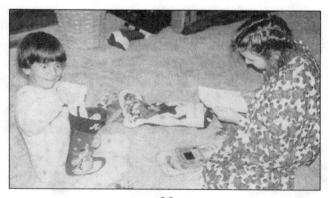

It was good for Hannah to have something beside the accident to think about. None of her friends were calling. She guessed that they all felt awkward about Daddy being so hurt. But she would have loved to talk to them on the telephone, even if it was just about simple, everyday stuff, like the presents they were hoping to get and how hard it was to wrap things really pretty. Or they could plan trips to the mall or to go to the movies. Mama was still very busy visiting Daddy, running errands, and keeping up with her work at the University. At night, she would fall asleep on the couch with her clothes on, even before Hannah's favorite shows were over.

By the Saturday before Christmas, Mama was doing better. Hannah was glad to see Kristi and Lauren at school when Mama took the girls to see Santa Claus. At least she got to talk to them while Mama interpreted for St. Nick.

Because Hannah and her sisters were leaving for Florida on Christmas day, Mama decided to let them open most of their presents the night before. Hannah wasn't sure about this plan because it wasn't how they had always done it, but she understood that they needed to go and see Daddy and then get to the airport in time to catch their flight in the early afternoon. Mama had recently heard a radio show about blind children and opening presents and she explained it to Breeze and Hannah. "This is what we'll do," she said with what Hannah thought was somewhat forced holiday spirit. "We'll call Daddy, and then we can take turns describing who is opening what, the color of the paper, the person's reaction, and all that to him over the phone, so he isn't missing out on it all." Hannah looked doubtful. "What do you think?" Mama finished.

Hannah agreed to the plan. They had to stick together and try to make Christmas the best they could this year. It was pretty clear that it wasn't going to be like it was supposed to be. "OK, Mama," she said in a quiet voice. "But there will be presents from Santa Claus Christmas morning too, right?"

Mama paused for a second before answering. "Right" she said, but her eyes looked off to the side as if she was trying to remember or think about something.

In Hannah's family, Santa Claus was never debated. Mama and Daddy believed in Santa Claus and they never wanted to hear what anyone else said. They knew that Breeze and Hannah tried to see if the wrapping paper used by Santa was different than the kind that appeared on the other gifts, and if the cookies and milk they left were really eaten, but mostly they just wouldn't debate the Santa issue. Still, Hannah wasn't convinced....

On Christmas Eve, the girls sat by the tree in the computer room and waited for Mama to tell them that they could pick a gift. Even if Daddy had been home, they would have taken turns, each watching what the other person opened. They had always opened presents that way, and it made the Christmas experience last much longer. But tonight there was another reason for taking turns and going slow. Daddy wasn't home, but he was on the telephone with them, waiting as anxiously as they were. Breeze took the first turn, describing Marcy opening a gift. "IT HAS..." she began. "Just a minute, Daddy," she said into the phone. "Mama, I can't hold the phone and sign, and keep track of everything I'm supposed to be doing here," she complained.

"I will interpret for the girls," Mama said. "You just describe everything as best you can for Daddy." And so that's how it went. Hannah got a Gameboy, and the little girls opened makeup and new dresses. Breeze was excited about her new piano keyboard. Mama never usually got presents, but this year Betsy, her friend from Pennsylvania, had sent her an apron with a pretty iris on it. Mama was thrilled. Inside was a note from Alliyson to Hannah, too, wishing her a Merry Christmas. Of course, she doesn't know about the accident, thought Hannah. Hannah wished Daddy could have been there to give her a big hug, like he always did after all of the gifts had been opened.

"LET'S HAVE SOME HOT CHOCOLATE AND GET YOU KIDS TO BED," Mama suggested. "SANTA CLAUS MIGHT COME HERE FIRST, YOU KNOW," her voice trailed off as she started to walk to the kitchen.

Hannah didn't want to wait up to see Santa

this year. Mary Pat and Marcy didn't say anything about it either. I just want to be in my bed and not think about all this, Hannah thought, feeling a little sorry for herself. She knew that Mama was trying hard to make Christmas nice, but it just wasn't. We are supposed to open our presents in the morning, Hannah thought, stomping on the first step, heading up to her room. And we didn't sing any songs, she thought as she stomped on the second step. On the last step, six angry words she didn't even know she was thinking escaped her lips, "Daddy is supposed to be here!" She burst into tears and flung herself on her bed. She sobbed and sobbed, feeling angry and sad at the same time. She didn't even hear Mama come in and was startled to feel Mama's arms around her.

"Hannah, what is it?" Mama asked, upset by Hannah's outburst. Hannah couldn't answer. There were no words to explain the confusion she was feeling.

"Is it Daddy?" Mama asked with concern. "You know he'll get better...he'll be home by the time you're back, honey...or is it about Santa Claus?" Mama seemed to want reassurance from Hannah that she was OK, but Hannah could only snuggle into Mama's arms and try to be comforted.

Poor Mama, thought Hannah. She knew Mama had tried her best to make Christmas feel the way it was supposed to feel. It just hadn't worked; it wasn't anybody's fault, really. Hannah wasn't really mad at Daddy, either. She knew he was just as sad to be missing them, laying there in that white, white bed in that lonely hospital.

"I love you, Hannie," Mama whispered. Hannah let sleep pull her down into blackness. She dreamed that Mama held her all night long.

Marcy tugged at Hannah's blanket, waking Hannah up. "SOCK, HURRY," she signed. Hannah opened her eyes and giggled at the sight of Mary Pat and Marcy jumping up and down beside her bed. It was a family rule that they couldn't go downstairs on Christmas morning until everyone was together.

"Come on, H," Breeze called from the top of the stairs. "Let's see what's in those stockings."

The girls zoomed downstairs and into the living room. There were the stockings, now to fat to hang, lying on the fireplace hearth. Hannah picked hers up. "SANTA CLAUS CAME," she signed to Marcy in relief. It was really Christmas! And by nightfall, Hannah was sitting with Grandma and Grandma Luetke, watching the beautiful Florida sunset.

Chapter 7

January

Uncle Bill had come from Montana, driving, Mama would tell them later, through freezing rain. His two Chesapeake Bay retriever pups traveled in the camper, bouncing up into the driver's seat every so often to visit. Uncle Bill often took long road trips, carrying everything he needed with him. He wasn't married and didn't have children, and he could tell tales that made any routine event seem exciting and new. Hannah loved to be in the same room with her mother's brother, listening to him talking. She liked the way her Uncle Bill took the time to explain things to her. He had that rare ability to talk about complicated things in a simple way that a little girl could understand.

Uncle Bill knew a lot about nature because he spent most of his time outside, hunting and fishing, hiking and exploring the western states. Before Mary Pattie was adopted, Mama and Daddy, Breeze and Hannah would spend two months every summer at his cabin in Montana. They would sleep in his little house or in a tent in his yard. Some days they would take long walks, play cards, invent games, and read. Other days they would hike up into the mountains and camp, cooking their meals over the open fire and sleeping in the cool, dry air. Sometimes they would drive half a day down to Yellowstone National Park to see the wild bears and moose. Once Uncle Bill took them in a big yellow rubber raft down the Stillwater River. Hannah thought it was a much better time than being at Oceans of Fun or Splashland in Kansas City, because it was real. Her family laughed and floated, sometimes going through white water and rapids as Uncle Bill maneuvered the oars and guided them along through the river cuts through the Beartooth mountains. Uncle Bill packed the best picnic lunches and never forgot the fishing poles! And now here he was, in Kansas, in the middle of the freezing winter to help take care of Daddy for two months.

Geez, thought Hannah, Daddy is lucky to have Uncle Bill. How many other guys would move into someone else's house for two months? Mama had explained to the girls that the doctors had refused to allow Daddy to come home unless there was someone there who could lift him. Daddy was much too big for Mama to manage and besides, Mama had to work and take care of the girls. So Mama had called her brother, Uncle Bill.

Uncle Bill didn't have a telephone, so Mama had to call the police in Red Lodge. The police had driven out to his cabin to tell him to call his sister. Hannah thought that he must have been scared to see the police car pull up to his little cabin!

Uncle Bill had arrived in time for Mary Pat's seventh birthday party. Mary Pat had already had one party while the girls were in Florida but Mama wanted her to have another party with all her school friends, too. Daddy would be in his hospital bed in the living room, but Mama insisted that Mary Pat have her school friends over anyway. "Good decision," Hannah had told Mama while she was making Bisquick coffee cake one morning. She liked that some things were getting back to normal.

After much discussion, Mary Pat finally settled on a bride party because she loved weddings and brides. Mama invited all the girls in Mary Pat's class and asked them to dress up in wedding gowns. She and Breeze planned games that included things like "who can throw their bouquet the farthest," "who can walk and carry a book on her head at the same time," and "pin the veil on the bride." The girls also played with makeup and had little tea cakes and punch in teacups instead of the usual birthday cake. Hannah thought it was one of the best theme parties that they had ever had and it had been fun to watch Mary Pat with all her friends.

Uncle Bill remained unimpressed. It occurred to Hannah, as she sat watching Mary Pat opening her presents, that she wasn't even jealous of her little sister. "I'm too old for that now," she said to herself. As she surveyed the group, she spotted Marcy. "Poor kid," said Hannah to Breeze. "She can't understand at all why Mary Pat has all the presents and is getting all the attention." Hannah moved over to Marcy, but despite her best efforts throughout the rest of the party to be especially nice to her, Marcy was sent to her bedroom several times, being "timed out" for naughty behavior. It would take a long time for Marcy to understand American customs, having begun her life in a lonely, faraway orphanage.

Like Hannah, Daddy was in good spirits for the birthday party. He was feeling much better and seemed to really enjoy being part of the action. The parents who brought Mary Pat's friends over for the party came into the living room and wished him well, and he was enjoying the first real company he had had since coming home some three weeks earlier.

Hannah was happy to see him smiling and talking. His face was all cleared up, the cuts and bruises gone. He still couldn't get out of bed, but he and Uncle Bill played lots of chess and watched football games on television. One night Mama showed videotapes taken when they had lived in Illinois and everyone laughed at how young and cute they all were then. Marcy had never seen most of these videotapes and it confused her to see her sisters at much younger ages. "That's me," Hannah would say and point to her younger self on the television screen. "See?" Marcy would make a face and look at Daddy for confirmation that it couldn't be so. Everyone was laughing and having a nice time and Hannah let out a long breath of air. Yes, sir, life was getting back to normal at last!

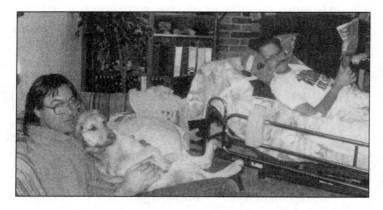

Uncle Bill was a wonderful cook! Hannah always hoped that there would be leftovers from the lunch he made for Daddy when she came home from school. The house smelled so good when Uncle Bill had the cooking pots out. He made pasta, fried vegetables, and something he called Alfredo Surprise, and would always explain to whoever was interested how he prepared these favorite dishes. Grandma Bette hadn't taught Uncle Bill to cook; he had learned on his own, watching friends and experimenting. Hannah thought that was neat.

Before Daddy's accident, Mama and Daddy were always watching their weight. No cream cheese or cooking with butter. Now Hannah was thrilled with the changes in the food around the house! There were always interesting things to eat and Hannah and her sisters would sit at the kitchen counter and giggle over bagels and cream cheese with their uncle. "So exotic," said Hannah with a sigh.

It snowed so much in January, Hannah couldn't believe it! She would wake up and beg Mama to listen to the news before they all got dressed. "It's so snowy outside, Mama," she would pretend to whine, "it's probably a `snow day' and I'm sure there won't be any school." Mama needed to work and wasn't happy about so many snow days with the kids home and the house noisy for Daddy and Uncle Bill. By midmorning, Mama would be trying to find ways to get the little girls out of house. The trouble was, with the snow, most of the fun places for kids to go were closed, too. Mama would try to get the girls to play outside. They were still at the age where they needed help getting all their snow things on—the pants, the boots, the hats and scarves. "SEE?" she would sign, "YOU CAN MAKE A SNOW ANGEL." Or she would throw on her own coat and go outside with them for a few minutes. Hannah watched her one afternoon as she began rolling a small ball of snow. "THIS CAN BE A SNOW PERSON," she signed, "BUT YOU CAN ROLL THE SNOW INTO MUCH BIGGER BALLS." She stretched her arms wide and smiled an enticing smile to indicate how much fun it all could be. But even if Mama managed to get the little girls outside, the Kansas wind would turn their cheeks pink and they'd be back inside to get warm in just a few minutes.

In Kansas there was also ice-rain. The little girls would walk out the door and slip. Bam! Down they would go and they would be ready to come back in. Mama was exhausted dressing and undressing them. By noon she was usually grumpy and Hannah would escape to her room to be away from her.

One icy snow day, Uncle Bill took the girls sledding. The puppies followed Hannah, Marcy, and Mary Pat as he gave them a push down the ice that had covered their driveway. It was so slippery that Uncle Bill would have to run down after them and help them back up the drive again, the puppies dancing all around the girls. Sometimes Mama would make them hot chocolate and they would do puzzles and play UNO. And even when it wasn't a snow day, Mama let them watch much more television than they usually were allowed and then she'd disappear into her bedroom. At first, Hannah didn't think too much about it, but then she started to wonder why Mama was spending so much time alone and was always crabby. Hannah was worried about Mama although she knew that Daddy's accident had made her life much more difficult.

One night Mama called Breeze and Hannah into her bedroom. "I want to talk to you about something," she said as they came through the double doors of the big room. They climbed up on the bed and sat facing Mama with their legs crossed. "I know I haven't been a very fun person to live with for this whole month," Mama began. "I'm not sure what to do with myself."

"Do you want to paint my room this weekend?" Breeze suggested. Hannah couldn't believe Breeze would say such a thing, but Mama's response shocked her even more.

Mama smiled as if Breeze understood her, "You know, Breeze, that might be just what I need. A project. What color were you thinking?"

"I want it to look like you are in a swimming pool," Breeze stated with confidence. She had obviously been thinking about this for a long time. "Then I want to decorate with all kinds of fish and shells and things."

"That seems a little drastic to me," Mama said in her "I don't think so" voice. "But...." then Mama smiled the first real smile that Hannah had seen for several weeks, "Let's do it!"

"Can I help?" said Hannah.

"Yeah, I think you're old enough," Mama replied. "Uncle Bill will probably watch sports on Sunday with Daddy, and we can take turns with the little girls, OK?"

"Sounds fair," agreed Breeze. "Can we go and get the paint on Saturday after our violin lessons?"

Mama, Breeze, and Hannah painted Breeze's room that weekend. It turned out so great that Mama wanted to paint Hannah's room the next weekend. They chose a shade of yellow that Hannah thought looked like sunshine, and Hannah kept the same curtains and bedspread she had loved for many years. And the Mama that she loved seemed like her old self again, too!

One day Hannah asked Mama if they could fix the fireplace in the living room. It had been a cold and empty brick hole when they moved into the house and now everyone agreed that it was time to fix it right. Daddy used his good hand and the telephone to find out how to fix it while Mama was at work one day. Uncle Bill and Mama bought the gas logs and then a man came to put them in the fireplace and connect the gas. Hannah loved the glow and heat from their `new' fireplace and she asked for it to be turned on every night. She liked to think that the fire warmed Daddy as he slept and made him feel comforted and loved.

"Do you like the fire?" Hannah would ask Daddy often over the next few days.

"I sure do, Han," Daddy would say.

There were several surprises for Hannah during the last week of January. One day she came home from school to find Uncle Bill scooting around the house in a wheelchair.

"What are you doing, Uncle Bill?" she giggled as she flung her coat on the coat tree in the hallway.

"I'm trying to see if your Dad can get around your house in a wheelchair. I think he can."

"With only one hand?" Hannah said suspiciously.

"Watch this." Uncle Bill moved the wheel of the chair with his right hand and it went a little crooked, to the left. Then he used his right foot, because the right side was the only one that her Dad was able to use, and straightened the chair back again. Slowly, he zigzagged his way from the entry way through the living room and out to the kitchen. "See?" he smiled.

The next day when Hannah came home, Daddy was at the front door to greet her. He was in the wheelchair!

"Wow," said Hannah. "WOW!" echoed Mary Pat.

"Did the doctor say it's OK to do that?" Breeze asked, concerned.

"Yup!" smiled Daddy. "I've been practicing with Uncle Bill all day. I can roll all over the downstairs here. It's great."

Daddy and Uncle Bill were so busy practicing with the wheel chair that Breeze decided to make chili for dinner that night. She asked Hannah if she'd help cut the vegetables. "Let's use the food processor," Hannah suggested. "Right," Breeze replied, moving quickly from the counter to the refrigerator as she pulled out tomatoes, celery, onion, and green pepper.

The chili was delicious! Mama was so pleased with the girls. "Thanks, you guys," she cooed at dinner. "We won't have much of this left over!"

"Great meal," Daddy said. He had wheeled himself to the table for his first meal with the family in six weeks. It pleased Hannah to see him eat so heartily.

Just as it was time to clear the dishes, the telephone rang. It was Jessica for Hannah. Aunt Susan and Uncle Artie had let her call to see how Hannah was doing. "Things are better," Hannah said honestly, as she carried the portable telephone out of the noisy kitchen. Hannah wanted to tell Jessie about how scared she had been when she had first seen Daddy in the hospital and about how Uncle Artie had taken them ice skating, but she just couldn't say much. Daddy was still not back to work and Mama still had crabby days. There was a lot to be worried about. How could Hannah explain it all so Jessie would understand?

"Hannah," Jessie interrupted the silence, "guess what?"

"What?" Hannah said, wondering if Jessie was just teasing her and would follow with "That's what!"

"My Mom and Dad said that you can come and spend a week with me in August this year. They said that you can come after you finish with violin camp!" The words rushed out and filled Hannah with excitement.

"You mean fly by myself? Wow, that sounds great!"

"We can go swimming and to the Wisconsin State Fair," Jessie said. "My Mom said she would take us to Wisconsin Dells, too." Hannah could feel Jessie's enthusiasm though the phone line.

"What's Wisconsin Dells?" The words meant nothing to Hannah.

"Oh, it's this really neat place where there are rides and shops and it only takes about an hour to get there from where we live. And my brother might be here, too. Or he might be at hockey camp, I'm not sure."

114

"We can play lots of tricks on Trevor if he's home," Hannah said, mischief in her voice. It was so nice to ramble on and on with her cousin and escape. The girls talked for a while longer and then Hannah decided she better get off the telephone. "I'll write you, OK, Jessie?"

"OK, Cuz," Jessie laughed. Both girls knew that they weren't very good letter writers. "Maybe we can call each other again and talk about the trip some more."

Hannah hung up the telephone feeling happy and lucky. She slid off her bed and started downstairs. Before she could decide what to do next, the doorbell rang. Hannah skipped down a couple of steps so that she could see through the glass in the front door.

"Lauren!" She opened the heavy winter door and felt the cold wind blow into the entryway.

"Hi, Hannie," Lauren said from behind the scarf that covered much of her face. "My Mom said you could come over if you want and we tried to call but your line was busy and we had to get going to do some errands, and..."

"Tell her to come in and shut the door!" Mama barked from the living room. Hannah was embarrassed that Mama would shout like that in front of her friend but it was getting cold, standing in the entryway with the door open.

"Can I go to Lauren's, Mama?" Hannah called back as Lauren came in and shut the door behind her.

"Yeah, sure, great," Mama said as she came out to talk with the girls in a softer voice. "Lauren," she added, "is Rachel in your car?"

"Uh huh," Lauren nodded.

"Would you run and ask your Mom if Rachel

can stay here to play with Mary Pat while Hannah is with you?"

By the time Lauren returned with Rachel, Hannah had her coat, hat, and mittens on. "Do I need my boots?" she asked her friend.

"Bring them so we can go out and play in the snow if we want to." Lauren decided as she helped Rachel take off her things.

Hannah kissed Mama good bye and followed Lauren out the door. "Oh, I'm so lucky," she thought as she skipped through the dusting of snow to the car. "It's a beautiful winter afternoon and Daddy will soon be walking again."

Chapter 8

February and March

*B*y his birthday in early February, Daddy was using a walker to get around the house. A walker was a metal support, waist high, that Daddy would set in front of himself. Then he moved toward it as he walked. He couldn't use crutches or a cane because his right elbow was still not completely healed and couldn't take the pressure. Uncle Bill was still doing most of the cooking, but Daddy was joining the family regularly for meals at the table. He had lost a lot of weight since the accident and it was fun to see him eat. "You certainly have your appetite back," Hannah would kid him as she passed seconds to him.

On Valentine's Day, Daddy surprised Mama by calling to have his hospital bed removed from the living room. From now on he was going to get upstairs and sleep in his own bed. He spent most of the holiday practicing on the steps while Mama was at work. Daddy showed Hannah when she got home from school one afternoon how he could hobble up the stairs using his one good side. Then he wanted a hug.

"I need practice with hugs, too." Hannah interpreted his request for Mary Pat and Marcy because Dad's good left hand was grasping the railing. Daddy hadn't been able to hug for a long time because of the surgery on his elbow. "Squeeze me,

Daddy," Hannah would coax. Daddy could get his arms into a hug but he couldn't squeeze much yet. Now, the girls took turns giving him hugs but Hannah didn't think they could ever hug him enough!

Hannah went up to her bedroom to open the Valentine cards that she had gotten that day at school. She read the notes from her girlfriends and chewed on little heart candies. Mama said she could have three friends over on Friday to sleep over, just like old times. Hannah couldn't wait. She wanted to play her Girl Talk game and listen to music. Mama said they could cook their own pizza, too. Suddenly Hannah thought of Mary Pat and the friends she usually invited over to play. They were all hearing girls and they could only sign a little bit. Mary Pat and her friends could discuss what games they wanted to play. Cards were no problem either. But how will she really talk with her friends when she's my age? Hannah thought. We have such long conversations about so many things, with so many words. It'll be hard for her friends to be able to sign that well.

Daddy was talking about going back to work soon. Hannah couldn't believe it had been six weeks since his accident. Just the day before, Hannah had seen Daddy and Uncle Bill reading the newspapers, looking for a new van. They were going to get a used one that was smaller than their old van. Hannah would miss the little television and special features of the big van, but she knew that Daddy's accident and his not working for so long had been hard on the family finances. Hannah watched the puppies nip at the newspapers as Daddy and Uncle Bill discarded the pages. Those puppies are so cute, Hannah mused. They've gotten bigger since they've been here. Hannah's next thought caught her off guard a little bit. It came from nowhere. I bet Uncle Bill will be taking them away pretty soon. Daddy is almost well.

Hannah didn't want to think about Uncle Bill leaving so she wandered out into the hallway to find Breeze. She saw that Breeze was in her room but, not wanting to appear too obvious, she walked into the bathroom and fixed her hair for a few minutes, then walked slowly by Breeze's door again. Breeze was standing on her bed and dropping different things on the floor. It was such a curious sight that Hannah forgot about trying to look disinterested and walked right in.

"What on earth are you doing?"

Breeze was standing very straight, her arm stretched above her head. Then something dropped from her hand and bounced on the floor. "Well, we're having Science Olympiad trials this week in school. I want to qualify in the egg drop competition and I'm trying to decide what to use for the egg container."

"What are the rules?" Hannah asked, curious.

"You have to wrap an egg in something so it won't break. It has to drop from high up. I don't know.....maybe about ten feet. When it lands, you don't want it to bounce because they subtract points for that."

Hannah imagined a tree trimmer in a contraption like she had seen in the neighborhood when people were getting their trees trimmed. She could envision this crane in a high school gym, with a man standing in it, dropping the student's projects to the floor, far below. "After they check that the egg hasn't broken," Breeze was saying, "they measure where it hits and how far it bounces."

"And the egg that isn't cracked and doesn't bounce much wins, right?" Hannah asked, her eyes already checking the room for materials that could assist Breeze. Someday she wanted to do the Science Olympiad, too.

As the girls dropped different materials from different heights, Breeze told Hannah about the other Science Olympiad events as well and how her teammates had scored in practice.

"I think my best event will be Astronomy," Breeze replied confidently. "Todd and I are both really good at constellations."

Hannah knew that Todd often called Breeze to arrange times that his mother could drive the two students to the observatory at the Kansas City Children's Museum, but she couldn't resist the opportunity to tease her sis.

"Is that why Todd calls you all the time?" Hannah said with a smirk on her face, her head tilted quizzically.

"Oh, right, H," Breeze retorted. She had no interest in dating boys but preferred to go out with her friends in larger groups. Her voice was serious with concentration, "No, really, we've memorized both the winter and summer stars and now we're working on the spring and fall constellations."

"Did you ever do a science fair project when you were in fifth or sixth grade?" Hannah said suddenly, thinking about some of the conversations she had heard from the older students in the Scarborough cafeteria. Hannah climbed down from the chair and started to gather up all the things that she and Breeze had been dropping.

"No, we moved here at the wrong time for all that stuff," Breeze explained. "They started it in seventh grade in Illinois and we moved right before my seventh-grade year. Here the Kansas kids do it in fifth and sixth grade and so I missed it."

"Too bad," Hannah said with sincerity. She was really looking forward to participating in the Science Fair next year. "I'm going to ask Daddy to take me over to Scarborough when the kids show their projects."

Hannah had a good thought. "You could come along and maybe help me with my project, Breezer," she offered, calling Breeze by her family nickname.

Breeze was in a generous mood, too. "Maybe....hey, I've been meaning to ask you...do you want to come to one of my swim meets? There aren't very many freshman trying out for the team - I hope I make it!"

"Is a freshman a ninth grader?" Hannah asked.

"Yup, and there are only eight of us trying out for the team."

"Is it all girls? You don't have to swim with the boys, do you?"

"No, H." Breeze smiled. "High school sports don't work that way. There is a boys' team and a girls' team." And then just to make sure that Hannah understood, she added, "Boys can't swim on the girls' team."

"And will you get a letter?"

"Oh, gee, I don't know," Breeze climbed down and sat on the floor beside Hannah. Hannah knew from overhearing Breeze talking with her friends that she really wanted to swim well, and that she loved working out with the high school

121

girls. "I'd be thrilled, really, just to make the JV team."

"What's that?" Hannah asked.

"It's the initials for 'junior varsity,' you dork," Breeze said rolling over onto Hannah. The girls had been serious for too long and Hannah giggled and wiggled under Breeze's weight.

"Aaaaaaahhhhhhhh, get off me. I'll yell for Mama. Please. Please...." Hannah was trying everything to get Breeze to stop her smasher hug. When her big sister began to tickle her, Hannah yelped, "Please stop. Please stop." She sounded like a robot, but the words had special meaning in her family. Long ago, Daddy had made a rule that when those two words were uttered, they were to be respected, and there was to be no more tickling. No one liked to be tickled when they felt like they could not get control of the situation again. Everyone agreed. Breeze promptly rolled off Hannah.

"Think I'll go read with Marcy," Hannah said, jumping to her feet and escaping the room. Mama and Daddy had recently asked the girls to spend time each day working with Marcy. Everyone had different tasks that they were to do. Mary Pat demonstrated log rolls, hopping on one foot, and walking on a balance beam that Daddy had set up in the basement. Breeze worked on English-related activities, like using prepositions and verbs in short sentences when Marcy was playing or dressing. Hannah's job was to read two stories a day to her littlest sister.

When Mary Pat saw Hannah spending time with Marcy, she interrupted their story time. "WILL YOU READ TO ME, TOO?" Mary Pat asked.

"TONIGHT," Hannah responded and went

back to trying to hold the book and sign to her littlest sister.

"OK," Mary Pat said, satisfied that Hannah still loved her, too.

That night Hannah read Mary Pat a chapter from Little House on the Prairie. "THIS IS THE KIND OF BOOKS YOU'LL READ IN FOURTH GRADE," she explained. "CHAPTER BOOKS."

Mary Pat looked in admiration at Hannah. "I CAN'T WAIT!" she said and relaxed back into the pillows on her bed.

When Hannah got to school on Monday, she discovered that Mrs. Shartzer had decided that their whole class would team together for the Science Fair. The project was about food decay. The class set out five cups around the classroom and Mrs. Shartzer gave them five different fruits to put in them. She had brought a banana, an apple, a kiwi, grapes, and a pear. The fourth graders worked as one large group to document which of the fruits decayed the most over a two-week period. Every few days they would record how much decay was occurring with each fruit. Mrs. Shartzer showed them how to write it down in a log they kept. They would vote each time to see how many students thought which fruits were decaying the most. By the end of the experiment, everyone agreed that the grapes were in the worst shape.

Lauren, Kristi, and Hannah talked about the experiment often as they ate lunch or walked home. They all agreed that the Science Project interested them and they wanted to conduct individual experiments as fifth graders.

"Hey, have you guys read the Little House on the Prairie series?" Hannah asked, changing the subject.

"No, but I want to find a book by Judy Blume during library time this week," Kristi said. "I started it last summer, but then I left for Girl Scout Camp and never got to finish it. Hey, how are you guys doing selling your cookies this year?"

"OK," Hannah said slowly. She really hadn't sold very many at all. Mary Pat followed her around the neighborhood and of course, everyone bought cookies from the cute little deaf girl. It made her kind of mad.

"I have enough to get the patch," said Lauren, "but you know everybody on my street wants to buy their cookies from Rachel. Just because she's littler and cuter."

Hannah felt her face turn red. "It's that way with Mary Pat, too," she sympathized. She decided not to mention her thoughts about the deafness factor. In fact, she was ashamed of herself for even thinking them.

Thursday after dinner Uncle Bill made the announcement Hannah had been dreading.

"Think the puppies and I will be taking off this weekend," Uncle Bill said to the group, not really looking at any one of them.

"Really, this weekend?" Mama said, sounding a little panicked.

"I don't want you to go, Uncle Bill," Breeze said quickly.

"Kent is better now, he's going back to work," Bill said. "You guys don't need me anymore."

"BUT YOU'RE WELCOME TO STAY, " Mama started to sign, suddenly realizing that Mary Pat and Marcy would want to know what was going on. "UNCLE BILL AND THE PUPPIES MIGHT LEAVE THIS SATURDAY," she added to catch them up on his announcement.

"DON'T GO, UNCLE BILL," Mary Pat frowned. "PLEASE STAY." Then she smiled her impish smile and went over to hug him.

"NO," Bill signed, and then quickly looked at Mama and added, "right?" Mama nodded that he had signed it right. He had learned several signs over the last six weeks.

"IF HE WANTS TO LEAVE, GIRLS, WE CAN'T HOLD ON TO HIM," Mama looked at her brother, her eyes meeting his. "THANK YOU SO MUCH. WHAT WOULD WE EVER HAVE DONE WITHOUT YOU?"

On Saturday, Hannah helped Uncle Bill carry his gear from the basement to his camper. He had called his room "the cave." "Mama," Breeze called. She was helping, too. "I want to sleep in the cave when I'm in high school. It would be neat to have that room down there."

"We'll see," Mama replied and turned away. She was thinking about Uncle Bill's leaving.

"Are you worried, Mama?" Hannah asked her, watching her face.

"Everything will be OK." Hannah hugged her Mama.

"Oh, Hannie," Mama sighed. "You're so sweet to me, but, no, things are much better. Daddy will be going back to work part time next week and Uncle Bill is probably ready to move on. He's not used to being with so many people. I feel selfish because we all want him to stay but I know it's right for him to go home." It was still too cold to wear dresses in March and Hannah was getting pretty tired of sweatshirts and sweatpants, knee socks, and hard shoes. "I wish we could go some place warm for spring break," she said in the kitchen one afternoon.

Mama looked up as if in a fog. She was planning the Saint Patrick's Day meal for the family. Daddy thought it would be fun for everything to be green. "I think we'll just stay home, babe. Daddy just got back to work full-time, so he doesn't need a break right now. I don't have much more time off and I want to save what I have so we can get away this summer."

Hannah looked away. She didn't know if she felt disappointed or not. She knew that lots of kids stayed home over the vacation, but her family usually did something special. Something different. "It's good for Marcy and Mary Pat to experience different things, you know, Mama," Hannah tried.

Mama smiled sympathetically. "Why don't we make a list of all the things that you would want to do with your friends and see if we can plan well enough so you can do one on each of the five days of vacation, OK? By the way, would you eat green mashed potatoes?"

Hannah started making her Spring Vacation Special Activities List. "I want to see Home Alone at the movies and have a sleep-over. I want to go to Skate Town and to the mall. I want to rent some videos and..." Hannah stopped long enough to take a breath. "I, I want to do something special with just Daddy and me. Go to a restaurant or run errands together. Just the two of us. Alone."

"I think that's a great idea, Hannie. I think we'd all like to spend some special time with Daddy. It's been so long..." her mother's voice trailed off.

Hannah had a great spring vacation. She even found time to watch Breeze work out at the high school with the swim team.

Mama offered to take her and two friends to the mall. She worked on her laptop computer in the eating area while Hannah, Lauren, and Kristi browsed in the different stores. Every 30 minutes the girls would come back and check in with Mama. After a while they decided to join her for some nachos and Cokes. "Can I come with you on your next round?" Mama asked as they finished up their food.

"Sure, fine," Hannah replied. She wanted to show Mama a pair of bib overalls in the Deb Store.

"I'll pay half," Mama had said when Hannah came out of the dressing room a while later. "Those do look cute on you."

"Thanks, Mama," Hannah said. She had saved $20 from her baby sitting jobs, but she was glad Mama was going halvsies with her. "I love the feel of new clothes, you know?" Hannah laughed.

When Mama asked Hannah to watch Mary Pat and Marcy later that week at Skate Town, she agreed. Mama was being so nice and Hannah knew Mama was trying to be available to drive her around town and still get her work done. She was a professor at the University of Kansas Medical Center. Hannah had never been able to figure out what she did, though. For two years when it was "take your daughter to work week" she had gone with Daddy to his school instead of going with Mama. It was easy to see that Daddy taught middle school kids math and helped them with computer work. Hannah could understand when he talked about buying new software programs for the students at his school and trying them out to see if they were useful. But Mama's job did not make a lot of sense to her.

"I direct the deaf education program at the University, Hannah," Mama had explained. "I've told you that."

"Yeah, Mama, I know," Hannah signed. "But what exactly do you do?"

"I teach a course each semester to college students, help them write a big, long paper, called a thesis, go to the library to read and look up information for people, talk to parents of deaf children, things like that..." Mama looked at Hannah to see if she was following her. "I do different things almost every day, Han."

"Why do you have to go out of town sometimes?" Hannah wanted to know.

"People ask me to come and talk about what is happening in my field."

"Your field?" Hannah interrupted. She pictured the wheat fields of Kansas and looked quizzically at Mama.

"A field is a special area that people know a lot about. My field is deafness," Mama explained. "Principals and teachers want to know what other people have studied about the best ways to teach deaf children English, how to help them to learn to read, things like that. They asked me to come and talk with them about it."

"So you're kind of like a teacher like Daddy only you only teach once a week, right?" Hannah knew Mama came home after she was in bed on Monday nights.

Mama laughed. "You make it sound like I sit in my office and watch old movies most of the day! But, yeah, I only teach a class once a week. You see me with work all the time, though, right?"

"Yeah," Hannah said. It was true that her Mama often dropped them at the movies and then worked on papers at the restaurant next door until it was time to pick them up. Or she would take them to Skate Land and then sit at a table and read difficult-looking magazines, called journals, while they skated. Even at the mall she wanted to write on her laptop computer before joining in the fun.

"When you go to college yourself, Hannah, you'll understand better what I do," Mama indicated by the tone in her voice that she was ready to change the subject.

Hannah in college. Wow, she couldn't even imagine Breeze in college, much less herself. "I only want to go to college if I can still live at home with you and Daddy," Hannah announced.

Mama smiled. "Oh, that would be wonderful, Hannah, but I won't hold you to that plan. You'll probably change your mind by the time you're 18 and graduating from high school."

"Maybe Jessie, Rachel, Lauren, Kristi, Emmy, Megan, Lindsay and I could all go to the same college."

"That would be something, wouldn't it?" Mama smiled. "Want to help me vacuum the downstairs?"

"I'd really like to help, but I have a book I need to read for school," Hannah said with a mischievous smile. She knew when to move on.

Chapter 9

April

"*Y*ippee!" Hannah shouted as she hung up her Pepsi can phone. "Mama, Daddy....???" she bounced out of her room. "Rachel will be here Friday night!"

"Is that what Robin said?" Mama wanted to know when she met Hannah midway on the stairs, her arms filled with folded laundry.

"Yup!" Hannah nodded with enthusiasm. "They're going to start out in the morning, right after breakfast and drive all day. Just two more days of waiting!" Rachel, her mom Robin, her two brothers and her little sister were coming to spend the Easter weekend. "We can do an Easter Egg hunt, right, Mama?"

"Oh, sure! Robin's kids would be really disappointed if they didn't get their baskets." Rachel's family was Jewish but since Hannah's family had moved from Illinois, Robin had come to Kansas with her children every year for the long Easter weekend.

"What else will we do?" Hannah asked, a little worried that her parents wouldn't plan the usual trips to museums, the mall, restaurants, and the movies because her dad had just gotten back to work. But before Mama could answer, Mary Pat came running in the front door and up the stairs.

"RACHEL AND ALAN ARE COMING FRIDAY,

MP," Hannah informed her, passing her mother on the stairs. Mama moved up and around Hannah to put away the clothes she was carrying. "DID YOU KNOW THAT?" Hannah asked her sister. Even though everyone in her family signed, Mary Pat and Marcy sometimes missed things when the hearing members of the family didn't remember to sign everything they said.

"YEA," Mary Pat confirmed. "I SAW YOU TALKING ABOUT IT BEFORE. WILL THEY GO TO SCHOOL WITH US?"

One year Rachel had visited in Hannah's class, and Alan, her brother who was one year older than Mary Pat, had visited the preschool. Hannah couldn't exactly remember which year they had done that because Mary Pat had gone to preschool for three years. A lot of deaf kids did that - started school at a much younger age than hearing children. Anyway, Mr. Cox, the principal, had been nice about letting Rachel and Alan visit but he made it pretty clear that once was enough.

"NO, NOT THIS YEAR. THEY WILL BE HERE AFTER DINNER," Hannah added quickly so that she didn't have to explain about Mr. Cox. Sometimes Hannah got tired of adding all the details for her sisters and right this moment she wanted to talk about Rachel's visit.

"WILL WE DYE EGGS, DO YOU THINK?" Mary Pat asked. "I LIKE DOING THAT WITH ROBIN."

"I'M SURE WE WILL," Hannah signed back. "BUT I'M GOING TO ASK MAMA IF WE CAN GET DIFFERENT KINDS OF DYE AND THINGS TO MAKE THEM REALLY NEAT THIS YEAR. LIKE THOSE S-H-R-I-N-K-Y D-I-N-K-S, YOU KNOW?" Hannah asked, finger spelling the funny name.

"I REMEMBER," Mary Pat agreed. "YOU WRAP THE EGGS AND DIP THEM IN BOILING WATER." Then she added, "NOT MARCY."

"YES, MARCY, TOO. SHE LIKES TO DO THE EGGS, TOO." Hannah said with authority. "SOME-ONE WILL HELP HER WITH THE BOILING WATER. DON'T WORRY."

Hannah could see that Mary Pat was getting herself worked into a fuss about Marcy and egg dying. Since Marcy had been adopted, Mary Pat sometimes acted up to get the attention of the rest of the family. Hannah would have never figured this out herself except that Mama and Daddy had talked with her on several occasions and asked her to be patient and to try to spend equal time with both girls. "I understand," Hannah had assured them.

Hannah knew there were times when she competed for attention, too. Like when Mama took the little girls to the audiologist to have their ears and equipment checked - which also meant that they missed half a day of school and got to eat fast food - or when there was a special event at KSD and Hannah felt left out being one of the few hearing people there. Hannah would sometimes pout or sulk, just like Mary Pat was doing now. Things seemed unfair sometimes. Once Hannah had talked to Mr. Clark about how she was feeling. He was the deaf counselor who visited Scarborough School on Fridays. She didn't want to tell him too much because she wasn't sure how he would react. She began by mentioning a few things and waited to see how he would respond.

"IT'S OK TO FEEL JEALOUS," Mr. Clark had told Hannah. "YOU HAVE GIVEN UP A LOT FOR MARY PAT AND MARCY. BUT I THINK YOU REALLY KNOW THAT YOUR PARENTS LOVE YOU ALL. I

KNOW THEY WOULD WANT TO SPEND MORE TIME WITH EACH OF YOU IF THEY DIDN'T HAVE TO WORK...MAYBE THEY WILL WIN THE LOTTERY." Mr. Clark and Hannah had laughed about that one. Then he had added an important thought. "BUT DON'T YOU THINK YOU'VE LEARNED A LOT LIVING WITH YOUR LITTLE SISTERS, TOO?" he had continued signing. "YOU SIGN SO WELL. YOU HAVE HAD INTERESTING EXPERIENCES WITH A LOT OF DIFFERENT KINDS OF PEOPLE. PEOPLE ASK YOU TO SIGN FOR THEM, TO INTERPRET ONCE IN A WHILE. YOU CAN TALK WITH ME AND OTHER DEAF FRIENDS..." he smiled.

Hannah nodded in agreement. She was glad she had taken a risk and shared her feelings with Mr. Clark. All he had said was true. "AND," she added with honesty, "A LOT OF THE KIDS HERE AT SCHOOL ASK ME THE SIGNS FOR THINGS. TEACHERS SEEM TO APPRECIATE THAT I CAN SIGN WITH THE DEAF KIDS IN CLASS AND IN THE LUNCH ROOM AND AT RECESS...YOU KNOW—I HAVE LEARNED A LOT OF THINGS LIVING WITH MY SISTERS."

Hannah thought that being a school counselor would be a neat job. She liked the idea of helping people think about their problems. Sometimes the hearing counselor who worked at Scarborough would come to her classroom and talk to the children about how to communicate better, how to work in teams, and how to problem solve.

Hannah suddenly realized that the house was very quiet. Some of the kids at school thought that living with deaf sisters would make things very quiet at home, but they were wrong. Now, as she sat and listened she wondered where they had all gone. Before she could decide, though, Mama came popping in, the little girls following behind.

"We just went to get the mail," Mama said by way of a greeting. In Hannah's neighborhood the mailboxes were all together in a big metal box down the street. Eppy and Patch, the sheepdogs, had followed the little girls into the kitchen, too, and were sniffing around. Mary Pat began to shoo them back out into the garage. Just listening to her say the dogs names over and over and noisily pushing them out the door gave Hannah the beginnings of a headache. Quiet? Hannah thought to herself. Mary Pat and Marcy were anything but quiet.

"Have you practiced yet? Got any homework?" Mama asked.

Hannah frowned as she climbed the stairs to her room. She wished the two days of waiting for Rachel would fly magically by and it would be Friday.

Hannah discovered that school helped to take her mind off Rachel's visit for most of the day but the time she had at home to think about it after school was almost painful. On Friday Hannah met Marcy and Mary Pat in the entryway of Scarborough School just as she always did on the days that they didn't go to KSD. Hannah found Mary Pat easily and the sisters waited for Ms. Nettie to walk down the hallway with Marcy's group of little preschoolers. Then the girls went outside to wait for Daddy.

It was a beautiful April day and Hannah wouldn't have minded standing in the school yard for awhile, soaking in the spring warmth. But Rachel was coming after dinner and Hannah could hardly wait any longer. She found herself being impatient with her sisters. She watched them dancing around her in the front yard of the school, hands waving, giggling, and obviously enjoying the weather, too. Luckily, Daddy pulled up before Hannah said anything that she would regret later.

"HI, DADDY," the girls all said as they waved to him. Daddy turned off the engine of the mini-van and jumped out of the car. "HI, GIRLS," he signed back. "I NEED TO PICK UP MARKET DAY FOOD BEFORE WE GO HOME. COME AND HELP ME. JUST BE A MINUTE."

Just what I need, Hannah thought, disap-pointed, but she followed her Dad back inside. Market Day was a school fundraiser. Families ordered food once a month that was brought to the school to be picked up. Hannah knew that lots of the playground equipment at Scarborough had been purchased with Market Day earnings.

Daddy got his list of food that they were to purchase and Mary Pat and Marcy followed him as he went from table to table in the all-purpose room collecting the family order. Hannah decided to sit on the carpeted steps that lined the room and wait. She noticed that several of the teachers were pick-ing up Market Day food, too, and she watched them as they walked around the room. There was Ms. Hatcher - she did speech work with all the deaf kids - and Ms. Judd - she was the QUEST teacher. Hannah wanted to be in the QUEST gifted program next year. She had no idea how kids were selected for it, though. She just knew that QUEST kids got to go to a special room and do neat things, and she wanted to go, too.

"Hannah...Hannah?"

It was Ms. Hatcher, the speech teacher. "Hi, Hannah," she repeated. "You waiting for your Dad to get his food?"

"Yes," Hannah said. She liked Ms. Hatcher,

who had beautiful blond hair and a soft voice. "You getting Market Day, too?"

"Well, yes I am," Ms. Hatcher responded. "But I'm glad to see you sitting here. I've been wanting to ask you about something. I've already talked to Mr. Cox and I just spoke with your Dad. Would you be interested in coming to my room sometimes with Tara for speech?"

"Do I need speech?" Hannah said, suddenly confused.

"Oh, no," Ms. Hatcher laughed. "I'm just trying to think of ways to make speech a little bit more fun for Tara. I think she would enjoy it if some of the girls in her class came with her sometimes. And, anyway, you hearing kids need to learn how to face a deaf person and talk directly to them. Also, Tara needs to learn how to speech read better and ask to repeat things if she doesn't understand. So we could all practice a lot of skills...."

"But I can just sign to Tara and we understand each other just fine," Hannah said shyly, still not understanding what it was she would be doing in the speech room - but she was interested in finding out more.

"Well, I know." replied Ms. Hatcher. "Especially you, Hannah, you're a good signer. But many children who are deaf also need to work to improve their speech reading skills - you know, to read what you are saying on your lips and to use the hearing that they have to listen carefully for clues as to what you're saying. Most of the time we don't sign in my room. Would you want to come?"

"Sure." Hannah said, deciding that she would like to go and see what kinds of things Ms. Hatcher did in her room. She thought suddenly about a story Mama used to tell about Breeze when she was little. She attended a preschool for deaf children so they could see how she spoke and used English. She had come home crying one day because she wasn't ever asked to go to speech and she wanted to get speech stickers like the deaf children. Hannah grinned. "Thanks for asking me," Hannah said to Ms. Hatcher. "I'll have to ask Mrs. Shartzer, though. Will you talk to her?"

"Yes, I will. We can schedule a good time so you don't miss important work. And," Ms. Hatcher added, "if you do need to stay in your classroom, just go ahead and stay and I will always know you didn't join me because you had something important to do, OK?"

Hannah glanced behind Ms. Hatcher and saw that Daddy was paying for their Market Day food. "I better get going now," Hannah said as she stepped past Ms. Hatcher. "Thanks again for thinking of me."

"Ready, Daddy?" Hannah asked as she approached Daddy.

"Yup. Can you carry a box of this food, Hannie?" He handed her one of the two boxes. Then, before he picked up the remaining box, he signed to Mary Pat and Marcy to follow him. Once the box was in his hands, he could only communicate with them with his speech. This usually worked pretty well. Mary Pat could understand a lot by watching Daddy's lips - especially when she could figure out from the situation what he was probably saying, like "Stay with me, now...watch for the cars as we cross the street" and things like that. Marcy couldn't speech read much at all but Mary Pat would tell her in sign what Daddy had said.

In ten minutes the family was home and had carried the Market Day food into the kitchen.

Breeze was already having a snack. She got out of school about half an hour before the younger girls and always beat them home. "When's Rachel coming?" she asked Hannah with her mouth full.

Hannah glanced at the clock. "If they come by 7:00 it will be 2 hours and 15 minutes," she reported. Just then the doorbell rang. Hannah's eyes widened. The sound of the door bell made the lights flash in the living room and by the time Hannah reached the front door, Mary Pat and Marcy were there, too. The front door had been left open, the weather being so balmy, and there was Rachel, big as life. "THEY'RE HERE. THEY'RE HERE!!!!!" Hannah signed and then zoomed out to hug her friend. Oh, it felt so good! "HI, HI, HI," she said with a laugh.

Children were crawling out of Robin's van and by the time the whole family had heard Hannah's call, Alan, Leah, and Billy were laughing and stretching in the front yard. Everyone was hugging everyone and when Robin finally emerged from the cab of the van, Mama rushed over to give her a special hug. "Ten hours of driving with four kids in the car...you deserve an award!"

"Let's get your stuff inside," Daddy offered. Everyone grabbed a suitcase and, with ten people helping, everything was unloaded in two trips. Hannah and Mama had long ago figured out who would be sleeping with whom, so Hannah helped direct people to the various bedrooms.

"It looks like we're staying for a month!" Robin laughed.

"Oh, we WISH!" Hannah and Rachel giggled together.

"COME ON, BILLY, COME PLAY WITH ME AND MARCY," Breeze coaxed the little boy. Marcy was watching Breeze and waited to see what Billy would do. He had just turned one.

"Play?" Billy repeated shyly.

Breeze laughed. "YES, WE WILL PLAY TOGETHER, OK? MARCY AND I WILL SHOW YOU WHERE THE TOYS ARE." Breeze turned to Leah. "Want to come, too?"

"Mary Pat, too?" Leah almost whispered the question. She was three years old.

Breeze glanced around and saw that Mary Pat was standing in the kitchen, already whining to Mama. "CAN I PLAY, TOO?"

Before Mama could respond, Breeze interrupted. "MARY PAT, LEAH WANTS YOU TO PLAY WITH US IN THE BASEMENT. MAYBE SHE WOULD LIKE TO DRESS UP WITH YOU." Breeze knew that putting on fancy dresses and silly hats was one of Mary Pat's favorite pastimes. She was willing to help distract the littler children so Hannah could talk with Rachel. Hannah was watching Mary Pat without saying a word. She was hoping to get some special time alone with Rachel.

Breeze's strategy worked. Mary Pat moved toward Billy, Leah, and Marcy, and as she did, the group of little ones started toward the basement door. There was a big playroom in the basement, carpeted and filled with dolls, toys, books, and costumes. Hannah sighed in relief.

"Thanks, Breeze," Robin sighed in appreciation. "It'll be nice to just sit in the kitchen for awhile without kids around."

Mama and Robin talked while they prepared an easy dinner of "make your own pizzas" and then called everyone to come and fix theirs. During Passover, Jewish people don't eat anything that has leavening in it. Hannah only knew this because

Rachel had explained it last year: anything that will cause things to rise, like yeast, had to be avoided during this holiday period, so Robin and Rachel used matzo bread for their pizza crust. Matzo bread is like a cracker, flat because it doesn't have yeast in it. Alan, Leah, and Billy were too young to observe the Passover tradition. They had fun choosing from the dishes of grated cheese, diced tomatoes and onions, sliced mushrooms and black olives, piling goodies onto their little pizza crusts. Mama stuck a tooth-pick in Breeze's when it was ready to go in the oven. "You're the oldest, Breezer, so we'll know that this one is yours. Rachel, you're older than Hannah, right?"

"Yup - by eight months!" Rachel said.

"OK," continued Mama, "So we'll give you two toothpicks." Mama stuck them in a big piece of mushroom.

When the pizzas had cooked, Mama got drinks and fruit and added them to each child's plate. "PICNIC," Marcy signed to her.

"YOU'RE RIGHT, HONEY. WE'RE HAVING A PICNIC!" Mama signed back. Daddy had arranged chairs and blankets in the backyard so that there was a place for each person to sit, and he came in to help the littlest children carry out their plates. There was a light wind blowing through the yard, but everyone managed to eat without plates blowing away or drinks spilling.

As soon as the children finished eating they raced off to the sandpile and swings. Laughter and giggles filled the air, and Daddy, Robin, Breeze, and Mama were left to relax and catch up on news from Illinois without children interrupting. They must have stayed outside for a good hour before the bugs started bothering Billy, Mary Pat began to complain about almost everything that Marcy did, and Hannah decided that she and Rachel were too big to be playing with the littler kids after all.

"Time to get ready for bed," Daddy decided suddenly. He got up and walked to the back of the yard, waving his arms to get the little girls' attention like the men at the airport who direct the planes. "LET'S COME IN NOW," he signed when he reached Mary Pat and Marcy. "TIME TO GET READY FOR BED. THEN WE HAVE A SURPRISE IN THE KITCHEN FOR YOU BEFORE YOU ALL BRUSH YOUR TEETH."

Like a mad rush of beetles, the children ran into the house. Everyone found their suitcases, and dirty clothes soon littered the floor as PJs were pulled over heads and arms poked out of sleeves. "ICE CREAM ANYONE?" Daddy signed to the first few to arrive back in the kitchen. "BILLY, YOU SIT HERE AT THIS LITTLE TABLE WITH MARCY, OK?" Dad said, clearing away the art supplies. Marcy and Billy sat down and Mama brought them each a bowl of ice cream.

"MARY PAT, YOU AND ALAN AND LEAH SIT HERE, OK?" Daddy said, pointing to the three stools next to the kitchen counter. The three dutifully climbed up and Mama served them their ice cream.

A good ten minutes passed before Rachel and Hannah made an appearance and only then because Mama went to bottom of the stairs and told them they'd better come down if they wanted ice cream. When they finally arrived they were talking to each other so Daddy just pointed at the kitchen table and they sat down. They were talking when Mama brought over their ice cream, too, and still talking after everyone else had left the kitchen to help the little ones brush teeth and get into bed. Mama found them still talking when she returned from putting Mary Pat and Marcy to bed. "Come on you two - time for bed," she said. "We have a lot to do tomorrow and I want you to have lots of energy. Hurry up, scoot!"

There was no way to delay bed any longer. Hannah and Rachel got up, put their ice cream dishes in the dishwasher and headed upstairs. Hannah was relieved that Mama hadn't raised her voice in front of Rachel but, much to Hannah's dismay, Mama followed them upstairs and Robin met them right outside the bathroom. It appeared as if the women were ganging up on them and Hannah knew better than to try to dawdle with two mothers watching. So she and Rachel changed into their PJs quickly, brushed their teeth, and settled into the trundle beds. Mama and Robin stood in the doorway and said good night, making sure that there were no flashlights, radios, or any other diversions tucked under the covers that would delay sleep. Much as Hannah wanted to keep talking with Rachel, her eyelids were heavy. The friends said goodnight and quickly fell asleep.

Hannah woke the next morning to all kinds of commotion. She could hear Marcy talking to Billy and knew immediately that her littlest sister hadn't put on her hearing equipment yet. Her voice was very loud and Hannah couldn't understand a thing she was saying. She doubted that Billy could either. Robin came in to check that Hannah and Rachel were up. "You two getting dressed in here?" she asked even though it was obvious that they were still in bed. "We're going to go to the mall after breakfast and then to a miniature museum. You might want to get going if you want to have breakfast today."

That was enough to convince the girls that they better get moving. "Let's wear matching clothes," Rachel suggested.

"OK," agreed Hannah. "How about t-shirts and overalls?"

In record time, Rachel and Hannah were in the kitchen, ready to eat. Dad was making pancakes in the shape of either hearts or dinosaurs and took their order. "The dinosaurs have no feet this morning," he warned. Hannah had used the dinosaur mold that Daddy was now using to shape the pancake batter and she knew that it was difficult to cook the dinosaurs without the feet breaking off. "I'll take a heart - maybe two," Hannah said.

"Me, too," Rachel said with a giggle.

Mama was cleaning up after the children who had just finished their breakfast. "Come sit here, girls, and I'll tell you the plan for the day." Mama seemed energized by the level of activity in the house.

Rachel and Hannah got their pancakes from Daddy, poured themselves a glass of grape juice and sat down. "What's the plan?" Hannah asked.

"Well," Mama started, taking a deep breath. "Daddy, Breeze, and Robin are going to run some errands, have a nice quiet lunch together, and set up the trampoline. They're going to take Billy with them. I'm going to take Marcy, Leah, Mary Pat, Alan, and you two to the mall."

"Do we have to stay with all of you guys when we get there?" Hannah asked with a worried voice.

"No, you don't. You and Rachel can browse and shop by yourselves as long as you stay in the same area as the rest of us. You can't buy anything, though, unless you come and get me. And then we'll all go to the arcade and Mr. Bulkies to get candy together." Mama paused to take a breath, "And remember to take the money you saved, OK? Then we'll drive downtown to the Children's Museum. There should be something there for everyone to enjoy."

"What about lunch?" Hannah asked.

"I think we'll pack lunches today so I don't have to take you all to a restaurant. We can eat in that nice park right across from the museum." Hannah groaned. "But," Mama added, "we'll give you each two dollars to spend at Mr. Bulkies and you can buy anything you want."

"YEESSS," Hannah and Rachel said in unison. Hannah wondered if Rachel had ever been to a store like Mr. Bulkies. There were rows and rows and more rows of big barrels filled with every kind of candy imaginable.

"And are we going to a miniature museum?" Rachel asked. "My mom said something about that."

"Well, I think we'll save that for tomorrow and take your mom, too. I think she would like to see it and we have a lot to do today already. We need to be back in time to get the grill out for dinner tonight and we still have eggs to dye and things to get ready for the Easter Bunny tomorrow..." she trailed off.

"Fine; great," Hannah and Rachel agreed. "Let's get going."

"OK, go get your money and meet us outside," Mama repeated. She usually told Hannah everything at least twice. "Everyone should be ready to go. I am," she said firmly as she got up from the table.

Saturday was just as full a day as Mama promised. Robin got a nice, long break from the children and Mama's group had fun browsing in the mall. The Kansas City Children's Museum had several interesting exhibits that really captivated the children. They all played in a room set up like a TV newscasting studio. Everyone took turns doing the news and then watching themselves on the TV monitors.   Hannah and Rachel helped Leah and Marcy at lunch, but otherwise they were own their own. By the time everyone had looked at the displays on the three floors of the museum, the group was tired and ready to return home.

Robin and Daddy were sitting on the front steps when Mama pulled in with the minivan. "And are we ready for you guys!" Daddy said in greeting. "Come on into the kitchen and let's dye Easter eggs." No one was tired, now!

Daddy, Breeze, and Robin had set up three separate "egg areas" in the kitchen. Daddy had a large pot of boiling water and the shrinky dinks over at the stove. When two children were at his "station" they took turns choosing a colorful wrap to put around the egg, then they dipped it with a spoon into the boiling water. As soon as the wrap hit the hot water, it shrunk up and molded to the egg like magic.

At Robin's station the children painted with a special dye and vegetable oil dip that made a marble-like effect on the egg shell. The eggs done by the youngest children looked muddy because they insisted on dipping them again and again into the mixture, but the eggs done by Alan, MP, Rachel, and Hannah were beautiful.

Finally, at Breeze's station, the children wrote with wax crayons on two eggs and then dipped them in the colorful dye. She had prepared five cups with vinegar and put two tablets of dye in each one so the colors came out deep and rich. Only Billy dropped his egg in a cup hard enough that it cracked.

For all the effort that Daddy, Robin, and Breeze had put into setting up the stations, it really didn't take very long for the children to rotate through them. In less than an hour all the children had migrated to the backyard and were taking turns on the trampoline under Mama's supervision.

Breeze and Robin cleaned up the kitchen while Daddy started to cook the turkey burgers that he had made earlier in the day. Rachel and Alan weren't sure they were going to like turkey burgers, so Mama ran up to Dillon's and bought some turkey dogs. Like the night before, the kids ate outside on paper plates, a gentle Kansas breeze cooling their picnic. By the time they had all finished with their dinner and drinks, it was 7:30 and too chilly to stay out any longer.

Now it was Robin's turn for a surprise.

"Everyone go get your PJs on, brush your teeth, and meet me back in the kitchen," she said as the children filed through the door off the back patio of the house. Breeze interpreted her request for Marcy and Mary Pat.

"KEEP YOUR EQUIPMENT ON," Mama told the little girls. Usually Mary Pat and Marcy took their equipment off when they put their PJs on.

"WHY? WHAT ARE WE GOING TO DO?" Mary Pat wanted to know.

"OH, YOU'LL SEE! VERY FUN!" Mama said with a mysterious smile. "HURRY UP AND GET READY FOR BED—PJS AND TEETH—SEE YOU IN THE KITCHEN IN TEN MINUTES."

As the kids reentered the kitchen dutifully outfitted in their pajamas, they saw t-shirts stretched out on pieces of cardboard. Tiny bottles of colorful fabric paint were pushed to the middle of the table.

"Have you ever painted on t-shirts?" Robin asked Hannah, Mary Pat, and Marcy. Hannah turned and interpreted her questions to the little girls. Everyone nodded even though they really hadn't. "We've made some pretty cool shirts in Girl Scouts, haven't we, Rach?" Robin added.

Hannah and Rachel worked together, each making very similar shirts. Mary Pat and Alan were perhaps too creative with the paint, but seemed pleased with the results of their work. Leah and Billy painted on one shirt that Robin convinced them they could share. The kids talked and signed quietly as they worked. The project seemed to have a calming effect. As each child finished, Mama and Daddy were on hand to escort them upstairs to bed. The fact that the Easter Bunny would be coming was mentioned several times and everyone went to

148

bed in anticipation of the Easter morning's basket hunt.

As might be expected, all the children were up at the crack of dawn. "YOU HAVE TO WAIT UNTIL 7:00," Mama warned them from the bottom of the stairs. "STAY UPSTAIRS UNTIL WE TELL YOU IT'S TIME." Hannah and her sisters were used to this rule because it was the same thing Mama and Daddy insisted on Christmas morning. Rachel and her siblings knew the drill from past years. Still, part of the fun was getting up early, standing on the top of the stairs eagerly anticipating what the Easter Bunny might bring.

"OK," Mama called as she stood at the bottom of the stairs and waved the "K" on her hand until both Mary Pat and Marcy had seen it. The little herd of children rushed down the stairs and out the back door, Daddy pointing the way to the hunt.

Breeze helped Billy, but the other children ran around the trees and play equipment until they each found a basket with their name on it. Mary Pat couldn't find hers and finally went to Mama for help. Daddy had just discovered that Marcy had MP's basket. "NO, NO, M, M," Marcy insisted, pointing to the first letter on the tag.

"I KNOW, HONEY," Daddy explained, "BUT MARY PAT'S NAME STARTS WITH M, TOO. THAT SAYS MARY PAT."

"WHERE MY? WHERE? WHERE?" Marcy signed as she reluctantly gave up the basket.

"MARY PAT WILL HELP YOU FIND IT." It took Mary Pat about 30 seconds to find Marcy's basket full of treasures. Marcy was delighted to have help because all the other children had been eating candy from their baskets for a good ten minutes. They sat in the backyard eating the pastel shoelaces, jelly beans, and assorted chocolates. As they ate, they compared goodies and played with the little toys that were tucked into the plastic grass.

Hannah was grateful that no one wanted to rush this Easter Sunday. This was her last full day with Rachel and she was going to enjoy and remember every minute of it.

Eventually the children wandered inside and got dressed. Mama went to the store alone and returned with food for a picnic at nearby Heritage Park. Daddy emerged from the basement with four poles and announced that they were going fishing. Off the group went to the park to fish, hike, eat, and play on the swings.

Rachel and Hannah took a long hike around the lake at the park. They felt independent and mature to be off on their own while the rest of the group fished. By the time they got back to the fishing dock, only Robin had caught a fish. Mary Pat, Leah, and Mama had wandered off to the swing set. "We're hungry," Hannah said to Daddy.

"There are some snack packs in our van," Daddy responded. "Would you run and get them and then take some things to Mama and that group. We'll finish up here in a minute and join you."

When the group had reassembled at the swings Robin broke some sad news to the girls. "I'm going to start the drive back home about 3:00 this afternoon, girls," she began as the kids started to groan. "You know it's such a long way and, well, to tell you the truth, it's just too much for me to do it all again in one day."

"WHAT? WHAT?" Mary Pat interrupted. She could tell from the expressions on the faces of the children around her that whatever Robin was saying was bad news. Daddy began to interpret for Marcy and Mary Pat.

"We never got to go to the miniature museum, Robin," Hannah coaxed. "Don't you want to stay and see it?"

"Yes, I do, Hannie," Robin agreed, "but we'll just have to go next time. You know we'll come back next year, right?"

Hannah was too sad to respond. "Come on, Hannie," Rachel said, pulling her up, "let's go back down to the dock and goof around until everyone's ready to go."

Hannah was glad to leave the group so she and Rachel could be alone with their disappointment. They had thought they were going to have this whole day to spend together and now it was being cut short. "Rachel," Hannah said quietly, "let's think of all the things we were going to do and figure out how we want to spend the time we have, OK?"

"Yeah," said Rachel. But the girls walked in silence until they had reached the dock. They sat together in the April sun and watched the lake water lap at the wooden dock braces. "Hannie..."

"Rachie..." Hannah laughed, softly interrupting her.

"I'm really glad you're my friend, you know."

"I thought we wouldn't stay friends after I moved," Hannah confided. "Did I ever tell you that?"

"No, but I wondered, too." Rachel said. "I have my school friends, just like you have Lauren, Kristi and the others. But you're my best 'out-of-town' friend!"

Hannah laughed and hugged Rachel. "Good thing we get to see each other in August at Violin Camp. It'd be hard to only see you once a year and stay such good friends."

"Rock'n Robin!" Rachel yelled and jumped to her feet. The girls watched each other to get the dance right, singing at the top of their lungs. What a racket! Good thing the fish weren't biting anyway!

"We could write more often..." Rachel suggested with a shrug as the two walked to the van. Both girls knew that wasn't going to happen. They just weren't the kind of friends who wrote and called each other. Nope, Hannah thought, we're the kind of friends who just see each other once in a while - but whenever we're together, it's just like we see each other every day! She found Rachel's hand and squeezed it.

Chapter 10

May

Lauren had called right after school to invite Hannah to sleep over the first Friday in May. "Can I go?" Hannah asked Mama, who was watching the news on TV and folding sheets from the piles of laundry heaped on the living room couch.

"Well, that would work out well," Mama answered quickly.

Mama's enthusiasm caught Hannah off guard. She had been preparing her speech to Mama all the way down the stairs. Usually a sleep over required lots more discussion and promises that she would go to sleep at a reasonable time, plan time to practice violin, do her Saturday job on Sunday, and so on and so on. But this time Mama seemed almost relieved to have Hannah out of the house for the evening. "OK for someone to sleep in your room?" Mama added, further confusing Hannah.

"What going on? Who's coming over?" Hannah was curious. She had the feeling she was missing something.

"Did you forget that this is Family, Fun, and Facts weekend at KSD?"

"Oh...yeah...well, I did." Hannah was expecting her Mama to tell her that she couldn't go to Lauren's after all. Hannah wouldn't have really minded that. She enjoyed being with Lauren, but Family, Fun, and Facts only happened once a year.

The staff at KSD planned an activity-filled weekend for all the families who had deaf kids. The parents went to a big meeting in the KSD auditorium and the children did special activities, too. Hannah's family had been attending this weekend at KSD since they had moved to Kansas and Hannah had made some special friends that she only saw on that one weekend each year. "Hmmmm..." she mumbled out loud, then tuned back in to Mama, who was still talking to her.

"Someone from KSD called and they need places for more parents to stay," Mama was saying. "They asked if we could take two single moms. Each has a little deaf toddler. I thought it would be a good experience for Mary Pat and Marcy to play with younger deaf kids. Breeze is spending the weekend with a friend so we can use her room. And we could put one family in your room." Mama didn't look up from her folding; Hannah wondered if she was expecting an answer. Lots of times Mama just decided things without much input from anyone else.

"Oh, well, it's fine with me," Hannah said nonchalantly. "They can use my room. So I can go to Lauren's?" Hannah asked again. "I'm supposed to call her back and let her know right away so she can ask Tanya or Sabrina if I can't come."

"Yup, you can," said Mama. "I want your room picked up before you leave, though, and you need to be home by about 8:30 tomorrow morning to catch a ride with Daddy to KSD. I'm going over earlier."

"I'll miss breakfast there, huh?" Hannah said licking her lips and remembering that Mama often referred to the special weekend as Family, Fun, Facts, and FOOD. The cooks at KSD fixed up the most delicious meals. Everyone sat together in the big dining hall and ate and ate. Hannah would miss that breakfast.

"You can make up for it at lunch," Mama looked up with a smile on her face. "Here, run these sheets up to your room for me, will you?"

Hannah grabbed the sheets and exited the room quickly. She suspected that if she stayed a minute longer she'd be asked to change the sheets on her bed as well.

Hannah and Lauren had a great time eating dinner and watching a video. After they practiced pitching, Lauren showed Hannah how to braid a "friendship" bracelet for her wrist. Lauren already wore three on one wrist and was making one for her little sister, Morgan. Hannah got a good start on the braiding but was feeling tired and ready for bed. She started to explain about KSD and the special weekend to Lauren in an attempt to suggest that they get some sleep.

"Family, Fun, and Facts—FFF," Lauren had said. Both the girls laughed.

"Yeah," said Hannah, "I gotta go to KSD for FFF—and F. Food!"

"Good idea!" Lauren giggled. The girls got a snack of popcorn, then cleaned up the bracelet stuff and got ready for bed. It was around 10:30 when they threw their sleeping bags on the family room floor and arranged an alarm clock and some stuffed bears for the night.

Morgan woke them up for breakfast on Saturday. "Hi 'Nah. Hi 'Nah," Morgan called to Hannah to wake her. "Ma's making 'cakes. You want'm? 'Nah?"

"Morgan!" Lauren complained, "Leave Hannah alone, pleeeease?"

"We'll come and get some pancakes in a few minutes, Morgie," Hannah said kindly. "Come on, Lauren, let's get up. Can I borrow your blue and green tie-dyed shirt for the day?"

"Sure, yeah," said Lauren. "Are you excited about going over to KSD?"

"Well, I met some girls there last year who were pretty nice, Talia and Erica. I'm hoping that they'll come again this year."

The girls talked as they dressed and then joined Morgan and the other members of Lauren's family for breakfast. After breakfast, Ed, Lauren's dad, took Hannah home.

"Hi, Hannie," Daddy called when she came in. "You all ready to go? Mama and the little girls already left with our guests. I want to leave in just a minute or so."

"Daddy, slow down," Hannah complained. Too much coffee, she thought to herself. "Yes, I'm pretty ready. Need to run and get a hair tie. Be back in a minute...." Hannah ran up the steps, just about tripping over the toys that littered the upstairs. The toddlers, Hannah thought. Looks like everyone had a fun time, she laughed out loud as she threw her overnight bag in her room and headed for the bathroom.

This year's FFF lived up to the previous years. Erica and Talia both came with their families and Hannah resumed her friendship with them immediately. By lunch they were sharing stories about school, parents, and sisters. Talia lived in rural Kansas and her sister, Tina, was the only deaf child in their school. Tina had an interpreter but was having a hard time learning in a first-grade classroom. Hannah thought about Marcy as Talia talked about her sister having to work so hard in the

156

evenings with her parents to keep up in school. Would it be like that for Marcy?

Erica also lived in a rural area—Anthony, Kansas. Her sister was hard-of-hearing and the family didn't sign much. Her name was Sabrina and she was the same age as Mary Pat. In fact, they were good friends, too. Erica was feeling a little out of place at KSD because everyone was talking about deafness and signing and she didn't have much experience with those things. "People think my sister can hear when she wants to," Erica told Hannah and Talia, "but a lot of times she really misses things. She gets frustrated and tired after a full day of watching the teacher's lips and trying to hear in a noisy classroom."

Mr. Clark, the counselor who sometimes visited at Scarborough, came to visit their group. Hannah introduced him to her friends. Neither Talia or Erica had ever talked with adults who were deaf. Hannah told them about the Christmas party Mama and Daddy held at their home with many deaf adult friends from the community. Talia and Erica weren't sure there WERE any deaf adults in the small towns where they lived. Right before lunch break, two deaf men stopped by the room where Hannah's group was working and talked with the kids for the next hour. One was Bernard Bragg, a deaf actor, who taught Hannah's group how to mime and incorporate signs into stories. Hannah thought that he had the most expressive face she had ever seen and she had no trouble at all signing to him or understanding his sign. When he asked Erica a question, Hannah interpreted for him without really thinking about it. She was used to interpreting in informal situations at home and at school.

The other man was Chuck Baird, a deaf

artist. Mama had a whole book of his art at home. Mr. Baird worked with Hannah's group to design kites that they would fly in the afternoon. As the children worked, Hannah, Talia, and Erica talked. Hannah felt comfortable with these girls even though she only saw them once a year. Just like with Jessie and Rachel and Lauren, she thought.

As the group got ready for lunch, Ken Clark stopped back in the room for a minute and asked Hannah if she would interpret one of the skits for the parent show. "WELL, SURE," signed Hannah to Mr. Clark. "BUT CAN I ASK ERICA TO HELP ME?"

Mr. Clark waited patiently while Hannah discussed the request with her friends. Erica didn't want to sign. "You sign well," Erica encouraged Hannah. "You'd do a good job by yourself, go for it." And she laughed and gently shoved Hannah back toward Mr. Clark.

Hannah had never signed in public before but she reported back to Mr. Clark that she would practice that afternoon. She decided not to say anything about it when she saw her parents and sisters at lunch.

The lunch line was long but it moved quickly. Hannah suggested to Talia and Erica that they not sit with their parents. Even Mary Pat and Marcy were sitting apart from Mama and Daddy today. They could be totally independent at KSD because so many people signed.

Everyone seemed to be busy eating and talking with new friends, held securely in the cocoon of the KSD cafeteria. Hannah went back for seconds and thirds on dessert. She talked with her friends and watched the younger children as they escaped outside to play in the sun, supervised by their parents through the huge glass windows of the cafeteria.

So many people all in one place who knew so much about living with deafness. All together for one long day of sharing, storytelling, laughter, and learning. Hannah watched the flying hands around her for a long while.

That night Mama and Daddy sat right down in the front row of the KSD auditorium for the parent show. Mama was videotaping as each of her girls came on stage to perform. Hannah and her sisters had been to KSD for holiday shows and graduations, Miss Deaf Kansas performances and talks, but this was the first time Hannah could remember that they had ever been up on the stage.

Mary Pat was tired from the long day of activities and did not behave well when it was her group's turn to be on stage. But Hannah giggled as she watched Marcy prance around proudly with her group of little friends. Finally it was time for the skits from the older children. Hannah took her place off to the side of the stage, apart from the rest of her group. She glanced at Mama and could see from her expression that Mama was wondering what was going on.

As a hard-of-hearing boy used speech to introduce their group's act, Hannah interpreted for him to the audience of hearing and deaf parents. It was just a few sentences but she felt nervous as she signed and looked out into the audience. Hannah caught Daddy's surprise out of the corner of her eye; Mama's face was hidden by the video camera.

When all of the performances were finished, Hannah and her sisters stayed near the front of the auditorium so Mama and Daddy could find them in the crowd.

"Hannah!" Mama and Daddy sang happily as they located her. "What a surprise! Someone asked you to interpret? Wow!" Hannah tried to pretend that it wasn't that big of a deal, but she felt very proud. Her face flushed with red.

"I'm lucky I can sign what that boy wanted to say," Hannah said, trying to sound indifferent. "And we practiced a lot, too."

"I think it was just great, Hannie," Mama sighed. "How nice that someone thought of having you do that. You ARE lucky...but not all the brothers and sisters here have learned to sign. You've put some effort into learning that skill, even if it doesn't really seem like it. Thank you for being able to interpret for your friends. I was proud of you."

Many people were trying to move out of the auditorium and out to their cars, and it was hard to hear what Mama and Daddy were saying. Mary Pat needed to be carried; she was just too tired to walk. Mama held Marcy's hand but it was too dark to talk with her. Marcy couldn't see Mama's signing until they got to the car and used the car light to make their communication visible. "DID YOU HAVE A FUN DAY, MARCY?" Mama asked her as she pulled her onto her lap in the front seat. Marcy nodded and flopped back in total exhaustion.

The women who were staying with Hannah's family had parked their cars right behind Daddy. They soon appeared, also carrying children who were sound asleep. Good thing FFF is only one day, Hannah thought. As late as it was, Hannah felt kind of sorry that the little boy and girl were asleep. Maybe I'll get to play with them tomorrow.

Everyone went from the front door straight to their rooms. Mama came upstairs to help Marcy get into bed and Daddy put Mary Pat down. He took off her hearing aid and plugged her battery into the recharger, but he didn't even bother taking off her clothes. Mary Pat allowed Daddy to move her through the bedtime routine, her arms and head hanging like a rag doll. It made Hannah even more tired just to watch. She was sharing Marcy's room, and took care of the bare essentials in her own bedtime routine herself before sliding under the blue quilt that covered the extra bed. As Mama bent down to pick up Hannah and Marcy's clothes for the laundry, Hannah thought to ask, "Are we going to Meeting tomorrow, Mama?"

"No, no," Mama yawned. "We're going to sleep until the kids wake us, get everyone breakfast, and help our guests get back on the highway home. Then we'll have a family day together."

Hannah turned over and closed her eyes. Sometimes she didn't like driving to Kansas City to attend Quaker Meeting, but she had wanted to see her friend Sarah there tomorrow. On the other hand, Hannah liked the idea of having an unscheduled Sunday with no particular plans.

"Night, sweetie," Mama said kissing the cheek that Hannah made available to her. "See you in the morning."

"LIGHT?" Marcy asked.

Mama flipped on the night-light so that Marcy could find her way if she needed to get up in the night. The soft glow from the little light didn't bother Hannah, who was sound asleep even before Mama tiptoed out of the room.

The next morning, Hannah woke to the cry of one of the toddlers. The little boy and his mother were staying in her room right across the hall, but the walls were paper-thin and it seemed like he was crying right into her ear. Wish I could just turn down a hearing aid, Hannah sighed as she listened to them dressing and packing for the trip back home. She felt shy about seeing them in the hall so she stayed in bed until she was sure everyone was down in the kitchen. Marcy, she noticed, had disappeared from the room earlier without waking her. That in itself was a miracle.

Hannah got up and stepped across the hall to her room. She peeked in the door and, finding no one there, grabbed some clean clothes and hurried into the bathroom. She washed up, changed her clothes, and fixed her hair before going downstairs. Oddly, she didn't pass anyone along the way; all of the guests and the rest of the family were in the kitchen. While the girls were eating Daddy's famous omelets and playing with the toddlers, Hannah scanned the Olathe Daily News for details about the movies. Maybe she could talk Mama into driving one way later that afternoon. Mama's probably pretty tired, thought Hannah. Then she noticed that there were lots of ads for Mother's Day.

"DO YOU REMEMBER WE'RE HAVING THE MOTHER'S DAY TEA THIS WEEK, MAMA?" she asked as Mama moved back and forth clearing plates and helping children.

"THAT'S WEDNESDAY, ISN'T IT?" Mama had just dipped the pans into the hot, soapy water waiting in the sink and little drops sprayed into the air from her hands as she signed.

"YUP," Hannah replied, aware that Mary Pat was watching their conversation. "THE FOURTH GRADERS HAVE A SPECIAL PROGRAM FOR THEIR MOTHERS THIS WEEK," she explained to Mary Pat and any of the others in the room who cared to listen. Mary Pat turned back to her breakfast.

"WELL, I PLAN TO BE THERE, BABE," Mama said. "WHAT WILL YOU BE DOING FOR US MOMS?"

Hannah went on to explain some of the recordings that the kids had been making to play over the public address system. It was hard for Mama to understand exactly what she was talking about and Hannah could see that she was distracted, cleaning up the kitchen and helping the mothers enjoy a pleasant breakfast. She decided that it wasn't worth trying to explain things in detail. Mama would see the special Mother's Day activities soon enough.

"Can you find someone to play piano for me on Wednesday?" Hannah asked Mama later on Sunday.

Mama spun around from the bed she was changing. "Why, Hannah?"

Hannah tried to sound nonchalant. "Well, Mrs. Shartzer asked if I would play a piece on my violin for the Mother's Day Tea. I thought it would sound better if I could have someone accompany me. That's how Ms. LaVonne always has us do it for recitals."

"Oh, my gosh, really? Play violin?" Mama started babbling and Hannah would have been embarrassed except that there was no one around to hear. "I think the high school girl down the street plays pretty well," Mama said, starting to think out loud. "Breeze has mentioned that before. What pieces do you have ready?"

"Bach Bouree," Hannah said, allowing a hint of pride in her voice. It was her 'polished' piece with Ms. LaVonne. "I've been playing it for a long time now and we've been working on some of the hardest parts at my lessons."

"I'll do some calling after dinner, OK?"

Mama promised enthusiastically. "I just can't wait to hear you play, Hannie. Have the kids at school— well, your teachers—have they ever heard you play your violin?"

"Nope, they just asked me because they know I take lessons. Most kids don't start with orchestra until next year in fifth grade so I think I'm just the only choice," Hannah added, trying to be modest.

The high school girl down the street agreed to accompany Hannah and Daddy drove her over to the girl's house to practice on Tuesday night. On Wednesday, Mama sat with the other mothers as the fourth graders sang several songs. She video-taped the performance to share with the family later and Hannah watched her as she sang, smiling into the camera. Mama was always videotaping things so Hannah had lots of practice in how to "perform" for the camera. There were three deaf girls in the fourth grade and Hannah realized that Mama was panning away from her to videotape them singing and signing along with their class-mates. Then Mama swept back across the whole group as all the students signed a song.

Hannah thought the audio taping the fourth graders had done was well received by the mothers. The students had each recorded a memory they liked best about their mother, and now their recollec-tions were broadcast over the public address system. A lot of the kids remembered times when their mothers had soothed them during illness or in the hospital emergency room. Hannah talked about the time she had fallen out of the top bunk bed when her cousins Bradley and Justin were visiting from Florida. Hannah had been leaning over the top bed signing to Mary Pat when she slid right off, falling on the hard floor! Listening to Hannah's story, Mama nodded at the memory of the black eye that Hannah sported for a week.

Finally it was time for Hannah to play. She was going to be glad when this part was over, she thought as she walked confidently to where she had placed her violin. Then she moved to the music stand by the piano and listened as the accompanist began to play. Hannah wasn't nervous; she had performed so many times with her Suzuki violin group that she was used to it. She played loudly and lightly and didn't miss a note. All of that practicing was finally paying off! Her solo was over before she knew it and she held her bow off the strings so the last note would ring. Then she bent to put her instrument away. When all the mothers started applauding, Hannah was glad she could look down, away from them, and into her violin case. She pretended to be busy until she heard Ms. Bowers, one of the fourth-grade teachers, inviting everyone for cookies and punch. As the mothers moved to the refreshment area, Hannah walked over to Mama.

"Oh, Hannah," Mama said as she hugged her. "You were great! You did a wonderful job." She didn't have a chance to say much more because other students and their mothers began to stop and congratulate Hannah, dividing her from where Mama sat.

Hannah smiled and said thank you many times as different groups of people passed. Mama stood back and let her answer questions about who her teacher was, how long she had taken lessons, was it hard, was she nervous, and so on. For one quick second, Hannah thought about how her playing had been compared to Breeze and realized that most of these people didn't even know Breeze! No, this was her moment and it felt super.

Of course that night Mama made Hannah tell Daddy all about the Mother's Day Tea and she showed the video tape to the whole family, interpreting it for the little girls. Marcy was happy to see Hannah in the film but did not understand that she had been the only student to perform a solo number. Mary Pat understood; she acted jealous by making noise and asking distracting questions so Daddy eventually sent her to her room. Breeze actually congratulated Hannah. She didn't say much, but Hannah was pleased that she said anything at all without Mama or Daddy having to ask her. Hannah went happily to bed that evening, wishing that tomorrow was Friday and not just Thursday.

The weather was so beautiful that Hannah

decided to ride her bike to school the next day. As soon as Mary Pat realized what she was up to, she wanted to ride her bike, too. "OH, MP," Mama warned. "DON'T YOU HAVE TO BE IN THIRD GRADE TO RIDE YOUR BIKE? WHAT'S THE RULE ON THAT?"

"THAT'S RIGHT," Hannah interrupted them.

Mary Pat didn't appreciate Hannah's comment and made a face at her that Mama didn't see. She's probably still unhappy from last night, Hannah guessed, wishing that Mary Pat would act a little more grown-up sometimes.

"TELL YOU WHAT, MP," Hannah tried to make her face look especially enthusiastic to match her message. "I'LL RIDE WITH YOU AFTER SCHOOL. YOU DON'T GO TO KSD TONIGHT, RIGHT? SO WE CAN RIDE WHEN WE GET HOME FROM SCHOOL. K?"

That was the ticket! Mary Pat gave Hannah a winning smile, grabbed her sack lunch and backpack, and pushed in behind Marcy, who was opening the garage door, headed for Mama's car.

"Thanks, Hannie," Mama smiled. "Easy to see you're almost 10! Have a good day."

Hannah grabbed her bike to get out of the garage before Mama backed her car out and closed the door. Patch followed her out but stopped before reaching the driveway as if he knew that he shouldn't leave. "Ten?" Hannah said out loud. Patch cocked his head, wondering if she were talking to him.

All the way to school Hannah thought about being ten. She needed to ask Mama or Daddy to buy something to share for a birthday treat before the school year was over. It wouldn't be long now...only a few weeks before school would be out for the summer.

Us "summer birthday kids" have to get our parties in May or June, Hannah remembered. It took a little bit of planning to have a school party at the end of the year. There were enough children in her class with summer birthdays and enough special activities at the end of the year that Hannah knew that she could miss having the kids sing to her altogether if she didn't plan it now with Mrs. Shartzer.

By recess she had scheduled a date with her teacher. Now she just had to think of a good treat and ask Mama or Daddy to pick it up at Dillon's. Maybe she would just ask to go along to the store so she could pick something gooey and chocolate herself.

When Hannah got home she had a snack and began to practice her violin. It was hard to be indoors on such a nice day; a warm breeze drifted in through her window along with the sounds of kids playing in the street. She tried to concentrate on her scales and sight-reading to make the time go faster. Hannah had discovered a secret: if she really focused on the notes of the review songs that she played, she would float into the music and lose herself. It was like taking a nap when her family was on a trip in the van. When she finished, she put her violin and bow away and skipped right down the stairs and out the front door. She played four square on the driveway with Mary Pat and Marcy until Daddy called them in for dinner.

Chapter 11

June

*H*annah was jumping on the trampoline in the backyard, watching Daddy. He was deep into one of his Sunday afternoon projects. Hannah bounced and watched, bounced and watched, playing games with herself to see if she could do certain jumps or splits before Daddy nailed another board. He was building a grape arbor. Hannah didn't know exactly what an arbor was but she could see that it was going to have four sides and a flat top. Mama would occasionally come out into the backyard to check Daddy's progress and give her opinion about the height of the arbor. "Not too high," she would say, "I want the kids to be able to reach the grapes." Hannah was interested in the concept of having grapes that she could reach, but Daddy had long ago told her to stop asking questions so he could concentrate on his measurements.

Hannah had her parents to herself today... a rare event indeed. Mary Pat had been invited over to her friend Mandy's house and one of Mama's students, Mary Bilson, had picked up Marcy for the afternoon. Breeze was off with her friends Amber and Jenny.

Hannah had the place to herself! No one had called her today to invite her to do anything and she hadn't felt like calling her friends, either. She thought that maybe Lauren was at Emmy's, or

Kristi had gone to the mall with Megan, but she just felt like hanging around the house and bouncing. It was fun to be alone with her games. Now she was pretending that she was a member of a famous drill team squad. That's what Kristi wanted to be in high school. Kristi had been practicing the splits for two years and took special lessons at Leigh's School of Dance in Olathe. Hannah asked Mama if she could take lessons, too, but Mama said that violin and Girl Scouts were enough activities in one week. "We've got four kids, right? We can only have each girl in two things." This had been a family rule for a long time, but sometimes Mama could be persuaded to bend the rules a bit. Not this summer though: Mama had just gotten her new license plate in the mail. It read "BLSTAXI."

Hannah hadn't seen much of Mama today. She was darting in and out of the house, asking Daddy his opinion on this or that, running back in, working up in her room, then coming back down for more advice. She was getting ready to go to Australia. Lucky ducky, thought Hannah. Mama was a university professor and some people in Australia wanted her to fly over and speak at a week long conference. Hannah had never been quite sure what her mother did all day long at work, but recently Mama was traveling a lot. Lynn Hayes, the woman who trained teachers of the deaf with Mama at the University of Kansas, was going, too. They were giving speeches at the workshop and then traveling a little bit around Australia before coming home.

Hannah hadn't seen Lynn since the morning after Daddy's accident. Wow, she thought, watching Daddy now it seemed hard to believe that he had been hurt so badly just six months ago. Now

he was using both arms as he carried wood, mea-
sured, hammered and sawed. You couldn't even tell
that his right elbow had been smashed or that his
hip had been broken in four places. Well, if you
looked really closely you could see that he couldn't
open his right arm completely straight.

He had been back to work for several
months and cooked dinner every night just like he
used to. Hannah knew he would take good care of
them while Mama was gone...although she couldn't
believe her mother was going to leave them for so
long.

It took 14 hours to fly to Australia so Mama
and Lynn were planning to leave a few days before
the conference to adjust to the time difference and
get over their "jet lag." Mama said that jet lag was
when you felt kind of tired and foggy and unable to
think very clearly. No one in the family had ever
been gone for three whole weeks. Mama was even
going to miss Hannah's birthday!

I'm celebrating tomorrow, though, Hannah
thought. She was taking gooey chocolate treats to
school. They were only having a half day and then
it would officially be summer! Right after Quakers
Daddy had taken her to the grocery store to pick up
her birthday treat so she'd be ready for Monday.
Mama wasn't very happy with her selection but she
let it pass. One day a year even Mama would toler-
ate junk food. Pretty clever of me, thought
Hannah. She had purposely waited for Daddy's
week to do the grocery shopping because Hannah
knew he would let her pick anything for her birthday
treat, regardless of nutrition. Mrs. Shartzer told
Hannah that they would sing to her for a break in
the morning. No lunch was being served at school
so it would seem like a big celebration when every-

one was dismissed just a couple hours later.

Good plan, Hannah thought. That was one of Mama's favorite expressions.

Tonight everyone was dressing up and going to Breeze's award ceremony. Lots of ninth graders who participated in choral activities would be there with their families. Breeze was getting an award for being in a special chorus that competed in regional and state singing competitions and for assisting the teacher, Ms. Summerour. She was also going to be performing a "Freshman Solo." Hannah knew the song Breeze had picked from Quakers. It was called "Everything Possible" and had been written by Fred Small. Mama had one of his tapes and she played it in the car sometimes. Breeze's friend, Jenny, was going to play guitar for her. Hannah bounced on the trampoline and watched Daddy as she sang the chorus of the special song:

> You can be anybody that you want to be
> You can love whomever you will,
> You can travel any country
> where your heart leads
> and know I will love you still.
>
> You can live by yourself
> You can gather friends around
> You can choose one special one.
> And the only measure
> of your words and your deeds
> Will be the love you leave behind
> when you're gone.

Daddy was singing softly along with Hannah as he continued to work on the grape arbor. Hannah was about to ask him if he would plan a tree fort with her to build later in the summer, but just as she was getting up the courage, Breeze and Jenny came out the back door. "Will you listen to us and see how we sound?" Breeze asked. "We've been over at Jenny's practicing."

"Sure," Daddy said, putting down his hammer. "I could use a break.... Hi, Jenny."

Mama came out of the house and sat with Daddy on the patio chairs. Hannah stopped bouncing and sat on the edge of the trampoline ready to listen, too. Of course she knew Breeze was in the special choral group at school but she had never heard her sing a serious solo. Around the house Breeze would sing silly songs with the little girls or sing rock-and-roll to the radio, but this was a lullaby that she had practiced over and over until it was perfect.

Hannah was glad that she was sitting quietly. Breeze's voice started softly as she sang the opening of the song and picked up confidence during the chorus. Jenny's accompaniment on the guitar gave the number depth and color. Wow, thought Hannah, she really sounds good. Hannah found herself getting excited that Breeze would be alone—except for Jenny—up on stage at the awards ceremony in front of many friends and their families. Breeze and Jenny finished and Daddy and Mama clapped. As they gave compliments and made some suggestions, Hannah jumped off the trampoline and walked over beside Mama.

Hannah wanted to say something nice to her sister. Why was it always so hard? The closest she could come to a compliment was, "Will you take the video camera, Mama?" Her voice was loud enough that Breeze could hear her and she caught Breeze's smile out of the corner of her eye. Hannah smiled shyly back

Breeze and Jenny left, leaving Hannah on

the patio with her parents, who were talking about the grape arbor again. It looked pretty good to Hannah. They were going to buy four grapevines during the week but Mama said it would take three years for the plants to get big enough to produce grapes. "Will they be purple or green?" Hannah wanted to know.

"PURPLE," Daddy answered.

"Daddy...." Hannah began, hoping she'd get a positive response to her next request. "Would you build me a tree house this spring?"

"A tree house?" Daddy and Mama both said at the same time. Mama's voice sounded disapproving, Daddy's sounded interested. Hannah's parents looked at each other in surprise. "Do you really think you're up to it, Kent?" Mama asked. She thought that just getting the grape arbor built was enough. "Hannah, not this year," Mama said before Daddy could answer for himself.

"Well, Hannie, I'll tell you what," Daddy said, beginning to contradict Mama. "If you sit down with me and tell me what kind of tree house you're thinking about, I'll sure consider it. And you and Breeze would have to be willing to help with some of the labor, too. That would have to be part of the deal." He turned to Mama. "If Hannah is thinking about something simple, nothing too complicated, I really think that we could build a tree house this summer. Probably just take a couple of weekends, and," he added, playing to Mama's weakness, "I think the kids could learn a lot about building from the project, too."

"OK," Mama relented. "It's up to you. Hannah sure can convince you to do just about anything, though." She turned to Hannah.

"Hannah, I want you to really think about

what you are asking of your Daddy. And if you talk him into doing this tree house for you, I do expect to see you out there helping. The weather is getting hotter. It could be uncomfortable. You think about it, OK?"

"Sure thing, Mama," Hannah agreed quickly. She was excited to help. "I'm going to draw some sketches right now so we can decide how much wood we'll need."

Hannah bounced inside before Mama could think of any more objections. This was going to be great, she thought. I'll call Lauren and tell her.

Luckily Lauren was home. It turned out that she hadn't talked to Emmy or Kristi all day. "Oh, a tree house sounds really neat," Lauren agreed.

"You want to come over and help me sketch some ideas?" Hannah asked.

"Can't, Han. Remember, we have softball practice at 5:30. For the Sluggers," Lauren reminded her.

"I think I forgot about that," she said, trying to talk and think at the same time. "I'm sure my Dad will take me...or I could walk down to the school...but I want to see Breeze perform at her school at 7:30. Hmmm, I'll go talk to my parents and call you back."

Hannah hung up and put her sketch pad aside. "Daddy," she called through her bedroom window to the backyard. "I have softball practice in 15 minutes. Lauren just said so."

"Oops," Daddy said, putting down his tools. "I forgot. Get your stuff and I'll go tell Mama that we'll meet her at Breeze's school after practice. Oh, and Hannie, grab something to eat quick, too."

Not long after, Hannah and her team members were assembled at the ball field near

Scarborough School. Lauren's dad, Ed, was coaching. It seemed like every girl in her class was on her team: Lauren, Emmy, Kristi, Tina, Katie, Abby, Sarah, and several others. Some of them had played together last year on a team called the Kittens or the year before that on a team called the Wild Things. Hannah still had those t-shirts.

Hannah was hoping she would be able to pitch this year, but Emmy and Lauren were really the best pitchers. Breeze had been a catcher when she was in fourth grade, but Sarah and Tina were already planning on catching. "Come play out in the outfield with me," Kristi called to Hannah. She waved at Hannah, indicating center field. Out Hannah ran, joining the girls who weren't playing infield positions.

Hannah caught one fly ball and missed a few grounders before it was her turn to practice batting. She was able to swing at several pitches before it was time for her and Daddy to say goodbye and drive over to the middle school. They walked into the auditorium a little late but found Mama and the little girls immediately. Because Mary Pat and Marcy needed to see the interpreter, the family always got seats right in the first row. Someone in charge would mark off a section with tape so the girls were assured that they would be able to see well. There was a deaf mother of one of the ninth grade girls who always sat with them as well. All Daddy and Hannah had to do was look for the interpreter and they knew that the rest of the family would be sitting close by. Sure enough, Mama had saved two seats for them.

Hannah sank into the wooden seat, her thoughts about the Sluggers fading quickly as she watched the ninth graders receive their awards and perform. There were several different choral groups: the Choraliers, and the Cougar Chorus, and the Corale. The names all sounded the same to her. She couldn't figure out the differences between the groups of young teenagers; middle school was so confusing! Finally it was time for the freshman solos.

Breeze and Jenny walked on to the stage. Breeze stood in front of the microphone and Jenny sat on a stool behind her. Breeze was right out in front, with 300 people staring at her. Hannah couldn't look; she closed her eyes and waited. Breeze started out softly as she had at home but her tune was right and she sang the words clearly. Hannah liked the way that her voice rang and vibrated a little on the longer notes of the first verse. Everyone in the auditorium was quiet as they listened to the message in the song and she saw that the interpreter carried all Breeze's vocal expression in the way she emphasized her signs. Breeze's voice grew more and more confident as she came to the middle and then the end of the song. She and Jenny finished exactly together and the audience clapped wildly. The song was a perfect choice for ninth graders who were leaving middle school and looking ahead to the new experiences of high school.

Mama and Daddy were clapping, and Marcy and Mary Pat were popping up and down in their chairs, waving their hands above their heads in the "deaf clap" gesture. Hannah clapped hard for her sister and joined in the deaf clap, too.

She watched Breeze proudly as her sister left the stage and walked down into a sea of friends. Ms. Summerour had to calm everyone down before introducing the next performers, but Hannah didn't

remember much after that. She sat and watched
Breeze, as her friends continued to slap her on the
back, congratulating her and Jenny. Hannah could
see that Breeze's head was bent and that her eyes
were downcast. She looks like I felt after my violin
solo for the Mother's Day performance, Hannah
thought. And suddenly she could remember all the
pride she had felt on that day. Breeze is too overwhelmed to feel it right now, thought Hannah, but
she will; just like me. And she smiled, feeling quite
mature and pleased with this sudden wise thought.

Hannah's party at school went well and soon
after she was walking home for the last time as a
fourth grader. Mama and Daddy had asked her and
Breeze to babysit the little girls for the long afternoon, until Daddy could get home from work.
Mary Pat and Marcy were in such good moods that
it was easy to get them home safely and feed them
lunch. Hannah decided to let Mary Pat help her
draw sketches of the tree house and they played a
few board games, too. The warm afternoon passed

quickly, the anticipation of summer evident in the air.

"WANT TO WORK ON THE TREE HOUSE?" Daddy said when he came in a few hours later.

"YES," Mary Pat and Hannah said without hesitation. They jumped up and ran out to the back yard.

"HOUSE? TREE?" asked Marcy, copying his signs without understanding what they meant.

"YES," explained Daddy. "YOU AND MARY PAT AND HANNAH AND BREEZE AND I ARE GOING TO BUILD..." and he stopped to mime pounding nails and carrying lumber... "A LITTLE HOUSE IN THE TREES—THAT TREE." He took Marcy over to the window and pointed to the big maple tree on the backyard lot line. Hannah and Mary Pat were already standing under it, pointing and gesturing.

Marcy ran out the back door to join them. She came running up to Hannah and repeated what she could remember of what Daddy had said, "DADDY AND YOU AND MARY PAT AND BREEZE AND MAMA AND ME BUILD HOUSE IN THE TREE! I EXCITED!" she signed.

Hannah laughed and hugged her. "YES, THAT'S RIGHT. WE WILL CUT WOOD, CARRY WOOD, HAMMER WOOD. WE WILL MAKE A LITTLE HOUSE THERE." And she pointed up to the limbs of the big, old tree.

"WOW," Marcy was overwhelmed. "WOW!"

The group didn't get much done that afternoon, but over the next two weeks they constructed the tree house after Daddy came home from work and on the weekends. It had a platform porch, four sides and a roof. There was both a ladder and a rope for going up and down. A second rope let children swing over to a nearby tree and come down that way, too.

When some of the Sluggers came over after softball practice a few weeks later, they agreed that the tree house was a pretty neat place. They were too old to use it as a clubhouse, but they wanted to use it for something special. Finally, Sarah and Tina hit on a great idea.

"We want to sleep in there!" Hannah told her parents after the girls had left.

Daddy laughed at the idea, "You hit a home run this summer, and we'll plan a campout in the tree house."

"Oh, Daddy," complained Hannah, "that's not fair. I'm not going to get a home run!"

"Well, if you do, sleeping in the tree house will be a fitting reward," chimed in Mama. "Otherwise, I don't want any more talk about sleeping out there. Too dangerous." Hannah could tell by the tone of her voice that there was no point arguing any more about it. She wisely changed the subject.

"Doesn't Mary Pat have a game tonight?"

"Yup, she does," Mama confirmed. "And we need to get going. Why don't you call Lauren and have her meet you out at the ballpark. Rachel is on the same team, you know."

Well, duh, Mama, Hannah thought. "I know that—but I'll call Lauren. Be right back; don't leave without me."

Hannah and Lauren had a great time sitting in the bleachers watching their younger sisters play ball. Mama and Daddy took turns interpreting for Mary Pat. It was almost as much fun to watch them as it was to watch the little girls. Interpreting for softball was pretty humorous. Once a foul ball almost hit Daddy and he had to jump out of the way. When Mary Pat was up to bat, the interpreter had to stand along the first-base line. Mary Pat's coach would mimic how she was to swing and then when she hit the ball, Mama or Daddy would sign, "RUN, RUN, STOP ON FIRST BASE... STOP...STOP!" Half the time Mary Pat wouldn't be watching them and you could hear her giggle as she ran. When she was in the outfield, the interpreter would stand as nearby as possible, trying to get Mary Pat's attention if the coach yelled out advice: "KEEP YOUR GLOVE IN THE READY POSITION. BEND YOUR KNEES." Half the time, Mary Pat was looking at the interpreter, but Mama or Daddy would wave, sign in huge sweeping movements, or run out and stand right in front of her, looking completely ridiculous. Hannah and Lauren had a good time laughing at them.

When it was Daddy's turn to interpret, Mama gave Hannah some money and asked her to take Marcy and Morgan to get a treat. Then she turned to talk with Lauren's mom, Julie. It took a while to walk to the snack hut for drinks and candy, but the evening was warm and Hannah passed several other games along the way. She knew a lot of the girls on the other teams and especially liked to watch the older girls play. When she returned, Mary Pat was catching. "Look, Hannie, look," Lauren yelled, poking her. Hannah followed her gesture, laughing, too, when she saw Mary Pat outfitted head to toe in catching equipment. She had fallen over trying to get a wild pitch and looked like a turtle on its back. The umpire had to lift her up and set her back into an upright position.

Ah, summer, Hannah thought. She laughed and poked Lauren back. "Well, Rachel isn't that much bigger," she giggled. Mary Pat was having a great time out there. Hannah was sure of that. And really, that was all that mattered.

Hannah and Breeze spent the first weeks of summer taking care of Marcy and Mary Pat. The schools in Olathe always started summer vacation a few weeks before Daddy's school in Kansas City, which gave the older girls an opportunity to make some spending money. Hannah spent most of the money she earned on candy and books; Breeze was saving hers for clothes.

Finally, Daddy was home for summer vacation, and Hannah and Breeze were freed of their babysitting duties. They went to the city pool sometimes with Daddy, but they also enjoyed staying home and talking on the telephone with their friends. They had lots of sleep overs and spent many nights at the homes of their girlfriends. It was all great for about two weeks. Then things started to get a little dull.

Mary Pat and Marcy started summer school. Most of the kids who were deaf or hard-of-hearing and went to Scarborough School during the school year went to summer school at KSD for three weeks during June and July. A little yellow bus stopped at the house each morning and brought them home every afternoon about 3:00. Hannah was very curious about KSD summer school. She tried to asked Mary Pat about what she did there but Mary Pat couldn't explain it very well. Hannah thought of calling Tara on the TDD, but she hadn't talked with her since the last day of school so she thought that would be a little awkward. Finally, she decided to ask Daddy if they could all go and visit KSD.

"I think that's a good idea," Daddy said. "I'll call and ask if it's OK and get a schedule."

Daddy picked next Tuesday for the visit. The little girls knew the routine well by now and got busy right away with their arts and crafts projects. The principal suggested that Hannah come by the nature area after visiting each of her sister's classrooms. "Ask for Becky," he said.

Marcy went wild, of course, when she saw them come into her room. Hannah discovered that Mary Pat was with Marcy for some activities as well. Classes weren't as structured as they were during the school year and the teachers and kids combined with various other groups for sports and hikes and special learning experiences.

Daddy and Hannah joined all the teachers and children for lunch in the KSD cafeteria. After lunch, they went to the nature center and met Becky Goodwin. Hannah was glad the principal had suggested they visit the nature center; it was a busy place. Children were feeding all kinds of different animals, looking under microscopes at things they had collected from the nearby pond, graphing information, and petting rabbits that were housed in pens out in the back.

"Do you think I could get a bunny?" Hannah asked Daddy. She decided he didn't think her suggestion was a very good idea because he didn't even bother to answer. Still, Hannah played with several different rabbits while Daddy talked with Becky. One group of children left and another arrived. Mary Pat and Marcy were in this next group and they asked Hannah all kinds of questions about the rabbits.

"ARE YOU GOING TO GET A BUNNY?" Mary Pat wanted to know. Daddy heard her and looked sarcastically at Hannah, but Mary Pat didn't really understand that kind of expression and she looked worried.

"IT'S ALMOST YOUR BIRTHDAY; ARE YOU GETTING A BUNNY FOR A BIRTHDAY PRESENT?" Mary Pat asked as if she had finally figured it all out.

Hannah smiled. Now, that was a good idea. "Daddy," she called, "could I have one of these cute little bunnies as a birthday present?" She really hadn't been thinking about her birthday, but now that Mary Pat reminded her, she realized that it wasn't very far away. Daddy just shook his head no.

"NO," he signed so both Mary Pat and Hannah would stop asking.

A little later, Daddy and Hannah left KSD and drove over to softball practice. They were going to practice together for a while and then Daddy would get home before Mary Pat and Marcy were dropped off by the bus. Hannah was going to walk home by herself. "Can Kristi come home with me, Daddy?" she asked and then quickly added, "That way I wouldn't have to walk alone and Kristi's parents are still at work anyway. She'd have to go home to an empty house...."

Daddy just smiled. "OK, OK, Hannah," he agreed, "but you really don't have to go through all of that to convince me. Kristi is welcome to come over."

Practice was fun. Hannah played second base as well as the outfield. There was a game on Saturday and the Sluggers were feeling pretty confident. Ed gave them all a few tips and sent them on their way. Kristi and Hannah started up the street, walking the three short blocks home. "What kind of birthday party are you going to have this year, Hannie?" Kristi asked. She was well aware of the theme parties that were famous in Hannie's family.

"Oh, I don't know," Hannah responded, "what kind do you think would be good?"

"What about a '50s party?" Kristi suggested. "You know, poodle skirts and saddle shoes and those sweaters that button down the front."

"Oh, yeah," Hannah agreed, picking up Kristi's enthusiasm. "We could go to this place in Kansas City that serves burgers, shakes, and fries...ah, Lucille's, I think it's called."

"Yeah, and come back to your house for a picnic in the tree house."

"And jumping on the trampoline," Hannah added.

"In our poodle skirts!" Kristi laughed, bopping Hannah on the shoulder.

Hannah could picture it, skirts flying up as jumpers bounced and the girls giggled. My birthday, Hannah thought. How quickly this year had passed. It's almost time to see Rachel and Jessie again. She turned in a circle on the front porch, her arms waving out from her sides. In just a few days Hannah would be ten; the family was going on vacation and another whole year would begin again. She turned a complete circle, just at the thought of it! "July, August, September..," Hannah sang out the months as she turned.